Melanie
AT
CAMP REDWOODS

What does a life-changing Christian camp experience look like through the eyes of a junior high camper? Join Melanie on her journey and discover for yourself why camp creates memories that last a lifetime. I highly recommend this entertaining and accurate depiction after twenty-five summers of serving campers just like Melanie!

—Jim Blake

Executive Director, Alliance Redwoods

In *Melanie at Camp Redwoods,* see the Lord open the heart of a spirited young girl as she experiences His handiwork in one of the most beautiful settings on Earth. I enjoyed reading the myriad of ways God worked for the good of Melanie. I cried near the end when Melanie realized how much God cared for her and how much He does for me, too. The story that started out as great fun became a great joy in my heart!

—Reverend Edward J. Crable

Pastor Hillside Alliance Church

The ideal blend of merriment and meaning, *Melanie at Camp Redwoods* is the perfect book for your daughter or granddaughter, but I should probably warn you, I predict you'll find yourself enjoying the story almost as much as them.

—James L. Rubart

Christy Hall of Fame author

The NorCal Girls
BOOK TWO

Melanie
AT
CAMP REDWOODS

J.D. REMPEL

Ambassador International
GREENVILLE, SOUTH CAROLINA & BELFAST, NORTHERN IRELAND

www.ambassador-international.com

Melanie at Camp Redwoods

The NorCal Girls, Book 2
©2023 by J.D. Rempel

ISBN: 978-1-64960-386-9
eISBN: 978-1-64960-385-2

Library of Congress Control Number: 2022944242

Scripture taken from the NEW AMERICAN STANDARD BIBLE®, Copyright © 1960,1962,1963,1968,1971,1972,1973,1975,1977,1995 by The Lockman Foundation. Used by permission.

Cover Design by Hannah Linder Designs
Interior Typesetting by Dentelle Design
Edited by Daphne Self

AMBASSADOR INTERNATIONAL
Emerald House Group, Incorporated
411 University Ridge, Suite B14
Greenville, SC 29601, USA
www.ambassador-international.com

AMBASSADOR BOOKS
The Mount
2 Woodstock Link
Belfast, BT6 8DD, Northern Ireland, UK
www.ambassadormedia.co.uk

The colophon is a trademark of Ambassador, a Christian publishing company.

To Jim Blake, Camp Director, and board members

Thank you for your years of service to Alliance Redwoods Conference Grounds (ARCG)

We appreciate you!

&

To ARCG workers, youth pastors, and camp counselors past, present, and future

Thank you for your dedication to the mission of Alliance Redwoods so that kids can learn about God and His wonders!

Returning Characters from *Melanie on the Move*

Melanie Cooper: Thirteen-years-old, talented swimmer, first time going to camp

Katie Graham: Melanie's best friend from the Bay Area

Cindy: Melanie's first friend when she arrived in town, who invited Melanie to church and introduced her to all her friends, loves to sing, and is very talkative

Haley: One of Cindy's group of friends, sarcastic teaser

Ella: One of Cindy's group of friends, sporty and muscular

Rachel: One of Cindy's group of friends, usually very quiet and soft-spoken

Bonnie: Melanie's Sunday school teacher, wife to Pastor Brett

Pastor Brett: youth pastor of the junior high youth group called God's Rock, husband of Bonnie

JB Barrett: cute boy Melanie likes, swimmer

Adam: bully, friend of JB's

Vivian: Melanie's neighbor and Cindy's voice teacher

Trevor: Cindy's older brother

Gretchen and Jack Cooper: Melanie's parents

Megan Cooper: Melanie's bossy older sister

Did You Miss *Melanie on the Move?*

Twelve-year-old Melanie Cooper is the star of her swim team, and her life seems perfect. But when her parents announce they will be moving to a remote cabin, her world begins to unravel. Melanie misses her father, her friends, her pool, and even her bossy older sister. She blames God for all their troubles. When her mom insists she attend church, Melanie ends up making new friends and hears the message that God loves and cares for her. But, she doesn't believe it.

Even though Melanie doesn't want to learn more about God, she wants to go to church camp with her friends, but because of their financial situation it's impossible. When her mother has a terrible accident, Melanie becomes angrier with God. But her neighbor, Vivian, challenges her with Romans 8:28: "And we know that God causes all things to work together for good to those who love God, to those who are called according to His purpose."

Find out the delightful surprises God has in store for Melanie in *Melanie on the Move*.

1

PACKING

Light streamed in from the living room window and from the skylights overhead of their A-frame cabin as Melanie stood in front of the large, golden, rectangular bird cage. Melanie poured fresh birdseed into Paco's dish, then refilled the grey-cheeked parakeet's water. Paco had been Melanie's pet for a couple of weeks. He'd been a gift from their neighbor and friend Vivian for Melanie's birthday.

Another wonderful present she'd received was a week at junior high camp with her new friends. Someone—an anonymous someone—had raised money for her to go, and the church had donated generously. Her best friend Katie would be there, too. She still couldn't believe it. Tomorrow would be the day she would leave for camp. A shiver of excitement coursed through her.

Melanie finished cleaning and then closed the cage door. Paco squawked at her and ran along his perch. He was great entertainment, especially for Mom, since she was recovering from her broken ankle and concussion. Mom rested on the couch while Megan, Melanie's older sister, heated up leftovers. Melanie went into the kitchen to help. She pulled down the plates and then set the table.

Someone knocked on the door. Melanie moved to answer it and found a package addressed to Mom.

Mom clapped her hands. "I hoped it would arrive on time."

Melanie brought over the parcel and plopped down next to her. "What is it?"

"It's for you. Something you need for camp." She tilted her head. "Go ahead; open it."

She ripped apart the wrapping. It was a box with a picture of a Bible on it.

"Oh, Mom. It's just what I needed. I was wondering where I'd get a Bible. I thought I'd have to borrow yours."

As she pulled the Bible out of the box, Melanie could smell the new leather. It was a dark blue Bible with her name engraved in silver on the bottom right-hand corner. She ran her hand along her name, *Melanie Cooper.* The pages were trimmed in silver.

"It's beautiful, Mom. Thank you." She embraced her mom.

Mom grinned. "I'm thrilled you like it."

"I more than like it—I love it!"

"You should thank your dad. It was his suggestion. He saw it on your list of camp essentials."

"Really?" Melanie could hardly believe it. Dad wasn't even going to church. But then, Dad was always so thoughtful and wanted to make sure his girls had everything they needed. It'd been so hard on him since he'd lost his job. But all that had changed when they'd moved here. They loved living at the cabin. Dad had found a job, and they'd made a lot of new friends.

After Melanie went upstairs to thank her dad and show him her new Bible, she went to her room to finish packing. She placed the box containing her Bible in her backpack; then she grabbed the "List for Camp" from the top of her dresser and checked the item off of her list. Now she had everything except her bathroom stuff and pillow, which she'd pack tomorrow before they headed to church. She'd gone over the list multiple times making sure she hadn't forgotten anything.

Melanie's favorite blue swimsuit was already in her suitcase, but with all the swimming she would be doing, it might be smart to have more than one. How many would she need? She pulled out another swimsuit from her drawer and then a third one just in case. It was better to be prepared, since she'd be spending so much time at the pool.

The microwave dinged in the kitchen, and Megan yelled, "Dad! Squirt! Dinner is ready."

***

Melanie and her dad entered the church parking lot. Parents and their kids milled around a large, orange school bus with their suitcases, sleeping bags, and pillows. Excitement bubbled up in Melanie. She was so glad her parents were giving her this chance to have the complete camp experience instead of dropping her off at camp, which would've been much easier.

After they parked, Melanie quickly retrieved her backpack and pillow and then jumped out of their SUV. Dad pulled out her blue suitcase and sleeping bag from the back of the vehicle. They headed toward the bus. While her dad handed Melanie's things over to Trevor, who was loading the baggage, Melanie stood in line to check in with Bonnie, her Sunday school teacher.

Cindy and Haley came up along beside her.

"Hey, Mermaid." Haley grinned.

"So, you guys checked in already?" Melanie asked.

They both nodded, and Haley answered, "Yeah, we've been stuck here since church let out."

"You have? Why?"

Cindy motioned toward her brother, Trevor. "Both of our families are going—Haley's parents and my brother."

Melanie had seen Trevor already, but she didn't know Haley's parents. How would she feel if her parents went to camp with her? Mom and Dad might be fun to have around. Now, if her sister, Megan, was a counselor, she'd definitely die of embarrassment. Melanie shook her head. She wouldn't have to worry; Megan would never go camping. It would be too rustic for her.

All her friends were here. Ella played basketball with some of the guys. And Rachel leaned against the church building with a humongous grin on her face as she texted someone. Who was Rachel talking to? She'd never seen her so animated.

A lady came up behind Haley, leaned over, and rested her chin on the top of Haley's head while wrapping her arms around her.

"Mom, you don't have to smother me; I'll see you at camp this whole week."

"So, you'll give me a hug whenever I want?"

Haley playfully pushed out of her mom's embrace. "Maybe."

Haley's mom made a pouty face. "Then I'll have to get in as much as possible since I don't want to embarrass you at camp."

"So, you'll embarrass me in front of the whole church?"

A big, tall man came up to the group. "I thought that was my job."

"Dad!" Haley sighed in exasperation.

Melanie looked at them quizzically. These were Haley's parents?

Haley glimpsed Melanie's expression and laughed. "Yep, both my parents are white. Surprise!" She threw out her hands. "I'm adopted. What gave it away? My Asian good looks?"

"Oh." Melanie didn't know anyone who'd been adopted—or, at least, she didn't think she did.

"It's no big deal. You can ask me anything about it. I don't mind, since you're my friend."

"Well, I was thinking you didn't look anything alike." Melanie bit her lip.

Haley's dad guffawed and pointed to Melanie. "I really like this one. She reminds me of someone." He stroked his bearded chin. "Hmm, now, who would that be? Oh yes, you remind me of my blunt and sarcastic daughter."

"Dad! You're terrible." Haley elbowed him. Looking at Melanie she said, "I guess I should introduce you. Melanie, this is my dad, Pastor Cliff, and my mom, Jane. Dad is the high school youth pastor, and my mom is one of the youth leaders."

Jane interjected, "Melanie, I've heard so much about you. Hal calls you Mermaid, right?"

"Yes, I'm the mermaid." Melanie grinned.

Leaning her head to the side, Jane continued, "You look familiar to me, too." She snapped her fingers. "That's right; you're Gretchen's daughter. I met her at Bible study. You look just like her!"

Melanie gasped. "Really? No one has ever said that to me before. Thank you." She blushed. "I think my mom is really beautiful."

Jane smiled warmly. "She is."

Melanie beamed. Haley's parents left, and the girls resumed chatting as they slowly made their way to the front of the line. Once they reached Bonnie, the girls moved aside to allow Melanie to get checked in.

Dad came over from where he'd been standing with a few of the other parents.

Bonnie held a clipboard and smiled. "Hi, Melanie. Hi, Jack." She scanned her list. "It looks like we have all your forms. Just give your bags to Trevor to load on the bus."

Dad replied, "That's already been taken care of."

"Then you're all set." She motioned to the bus. "Melanie, if you'd like, you can save yourself a seat and put your backpack and pillow on the bus."

After saying goodbye to Dad, Melanie climbed the steps. As she walked down the aisle, she ran her hands along the top of the seats. She glanced back and forth searching for Cindy's distinctive pink backpack. About halfway down, she found it and placed her own next to it with her pillow. The seats were on the side of the bus where she would be able to see her house as they drove past. Perfect. She could hardly wait for this adventure to begin.

2

BETHANY

As Melanie exited the bus, a silver luxury car drove into the parking lot.

"Bethany's here!" Rachel squealed and ran toward the car.

"Who's Bethany?" Melanie asked.

"She's the one we told you about at your slumber party," explained Cindy. "The one who is so infatuated with JB. She's Rachel's best friend. They're usually inseparable, except for the summer when Bethany goes to live with her dad."

They followed Rachel. Melanie bit her lip and walked a few steps behind. But Cindy turned and waited for Melanie to catch up and put her arm through Melanie's. A girl with long, strawberry-blonde hair and stylish clothes emerged from the passenger side like a celebrity. This was Bethany? No way! She looked way too old and sophisticated to be in junior high.

Bethany glided over to Rachel and threw her arms around her. "Bonjour." She then kissed her on each cheek. "That's how you greet someone in France."

Haley stammered out, "Why are you wearing such fancy clothes? You know, we're on our way to camp."

"Of course, I know!" Bethany raised her chin. "But this is my preferred attire, and I'm quite comfortable."

Haley muttered, "You are? Even wearing those high-heeled boots?"

"It's called fashion." Bethany whipped back with a superior tone.

Cindy shrugged. "Yeah, Haley. If she doesn't mind falling on her face, we should be fine with it."

Bethany pouted. "Guys, you're ruining my homecoming." She whined, "I thought you'd be more excited to see me."

"Oh right. Sorry." Haley scrunched up her face. "Just don't do that kissy thing with me."

Bethany hugged Haley, then Cindy. "Oh my, Cin, you cut your hair short. Why would you ever want to do that?"

Cindy's cheeks reddened, and her eyes pinched.

Strutting toward Melanie like a runway model, Bethany said, "You must be Melanie. I've heard so much about you, I feel like I know you already. I'm sure we're going to be great friends."

Without allowing Melanie to reply, Bethany abandoned her and hurried after her father, who was taking her designer luggage to the bus. The girls followed. After Bethany was checked in, her father gave her a bunch of twenties from his wallet and then quickly left.

Melanie couldn't believe how rich Bethany's family was. Everything about Bethany seemed perfect. Why would someone like her want to go to camp? It didn't make sense. She wasn't like the other girls either. Why did they all hang out together when they were so different?

Haley was the jokester of the group, Ella the sporty one, Rachel the shy one, and Cindy the talkative one. Melanie didn't know her place quite yet. But Bethany seemed like the leader. If that was the case, maybe she wouldn't fit in with her new friends anymore. Melanie bit her lip again.

A siren-like whistle screeched across the area, startling Melanie. "What was that?"

"That was my mom. She's got the loudest whistle," Haley proudly stated.

With everyone's attention, Pastor Brett waved his arm and yelled, "Load up."

When Melanie entered the old, orange school bus, she returned to the spot which she'd saved earlier. Cindy was right behind her. As she moved her backpack onto the floor, she said, "Cindy, I hope you don't mind but I'd like to sit next to the window. I want to be able to wave to my parents."

"Sure. That'd be fun."

Haley, who was in the seat in front of them, overheard. "We can all wave to your parents." Ella, hot and sweaty, agreed as she sank into the seat next to Haley.

As more kids trickled onto the stuffy bus, the air grew warmer. Melanie fanned her red face, but it didn't help. Hoping to cool off, Melanie pulled down the window. Others did the same, and a refreshing breeze drifted through.

Across the aisle, Bethany fussed. "Ugh, that's going to mess up my hair." She tossed back her lustrous locks.

Cindy relaxed her shoulders. "That's *so* much better. It was beginning to feel like an oven in here. Bethany, why don't you put your hair into a ponytail?"

Bethany glared at Cindy and smirked. "I'm really not interested in taking the advice of someone who thinks a boy's hair cut is a good idea. I care about how I look."

Cindy's face turned scarlet, and Melanie gasped.

"Bethany, could you *be* any nicer?" Sarcasm dripped from Haley's response.

Melanie leaned over to Cindy. "I think you look like a fairy. All you need now are some wings."

Cindy grinned mischievously. "If I were a fairy, I'd probably be a naughty one and put a spell on Bethany. She deserves to be turned into a toad."

The girls giggled. Suddenly, Cindy stopped and elbowed her. Melanie glanced up into the blue eyes of a smiling JB.

"Hey, Mel. It's great you made it to camp after all."

Her heart pumped rapidly like she'd just finished a relay at a swim meet. She hadn't talked to JB since he and his mom had visited their house a few weeks ago. When they'd last spoken, she'd mentioned she couldn't go to camp. It was sweet that he remembered.

"Yep, things sure have changed." She nodded, trying not to blush.

A musical voice cooed, "Hi, JB."

JB turned. "Oh, hey, Bethany."

"I'm so sorry I missed your family's Fourth of July barbecue. My father and I were in New York. He's trying to get me into modeling."

He raised his eyebrows. "Uh, yeah, no problem." JB hurried down the aisle to take a seat in the back.

Melanie faced the window to hide her grin.

When everyone was seated, Pastor Brett stood at the front of the bus. "Settle down, guys. We're going to pray."

The youth quieted.

"Let's bow our heads. Lord, give us a safe journey. Protect us in our activities. Open our eyes, ears, and hearts so we learn more about You this week. Change us into the people You want us to be. In Jesus' name."

"Amen," they all said loudly.

The bus driver closed the door, then tooted the horn. They were on their way.

3

CAMP REDWOODS

As the bus rumbled along, Melanie scooted forward and rested her chin on the seat in front of her. "Haley, I thought your parents were coming."

"They are, but they're driving our minivan. It's crammed full of stuff Mom needs for her and Bonnie's interactive seminar."

Cindy moved up closer. "Ooh, what's it about?"

"Missions and how we can help our missionaries."

What did Haley mean? Melanie had learned about the California missions in the fifth grade. Spanish priests had built them in order to convert the Native Americans. But this sounded different. It must be another church thing she didn't understand.

Melanie leaned back and listened as the girls continued to talk. When the bus rounded a familiar turn, Melanie sat up and patted Cindy's arm to get her attention. She peered out the window as they passed her house. Melanie and her friends enthusiastically waved at her family, who were waiting outside.

"Is that your family?" Bethany gave a bored sigh. "How sweet." Mockery seeped from her comment.

From the expression shadowed on Cindy's face, she'd definitely overheard and was annoyed. Melanie huffed and pursed her lips. She didn't like how Bethany was treating them with her insults and her haughty nature. But Bethany wasn't going to ruin her time at camp.

A few minutes later, the bus slowed as it reached their destination. A dark brown sign embellished with trees and bold white letters stated "Camp Redwoods." They turned into the entrance and drove down the slope into the parking lot, which was packed with campers who appeared as excited as she was.

After they parked, Pastor Brett stood up and announced, "Listen up. Please grab your registration forms. Girls, Bonnie has yours; and guys, get yours from Trevor. Once you collect them, head to the registration tables and get your cabin assignments. Afterward, meet back here so we can sort through the luggage. And, gentlemen," he said with emphasis, "we will be helping the ladies with their bags."

Several of the guys groaned.

Melanie hopped down the steps with her backpack slung over her shoulder. She could barely contain her happiness as she joined Cindy and the other girls in line. The majestic redwood trees created a canopy around them and scented the air with their rugged fragrance. After she retrieved her papers, Cindy and Melanie followed the others.

Turning her head from side to side, Melanie beheld the beauty of nature. The landscape at her home was so similar, but there was something different here, something Melanie couldn't describe. There was a feeling—one of magnificence and something more. What was it?

As they crossed a large bridge, Melanie stopped halfway. Then she dashed to the edge. Leaning over the rail, she peered at the water rushing underneath— Dutch Bill Creek, the same one which ran past her house. She giggled and twirled around.

"What are you doing, you goof?" Cindy teased.

Melanie threw her arms out. "I can't believe I'm here!"

"You're too funny. Come on." She grabbed Melanie's hand. "I promise as soon as we're done with everything, I'll give you a tour."

Melanie allowed Cindy to guide her, since she didn't know the way. Why had she been so hesitant to come all those years when Katie had invited her? The truth of it was that she thought church camp would be boring. What would they do all day? Sing and listen to sermons about God? Who would want to do that? But with her family's unexpected move, her circumstances had changed her view of Who God was.

He had shown her how much He loved her and cared for her family. With all the troubles they'd faced, He'd provided for them. And their church had become like their family—praying for them, preparing meals when her mom had her accident, and then raising money for her to go to camp. Now, she was here! It was unbelievable.

When they reached the registration tables, Cindy ushered her to the queue for the girls with the last name starting with A-G. As she waited, Melanie surveyed her surroundings. They were in a big, open area like a circular courtyard. Youth were everywhere, and the hubbub was filled with talking, laughter, and multiple activities. Skateboarders rode up and down a nearby ramp. A game of basketball was in progress over near the bridge.

When she got to the front of the line, the lady asked her name.

"Melanie Cooper." She handed the woman her paperwork as she'd seen the others do ahead of her.

The lady scanned her list. After she found Melanie's name, she glanced up and smiled. "It looks like you're in Berry Patch Seven. Your counselor's name is Bonnie." She pulled out a green, plastic band and clipped it around Melanie's wrist. "You are on the green team, and this is your meal ticket. Keep it on at all times. Your program booklet and t-shirt are available in the Fireside Room, which is the building behind me. Have a wonderful week."

Melanie raised her eyebrows. "I was wondering— has Katie Graham checked in?"

She scanned her list. "Hmm. Not yet."

"What cabin is she in?"

The woman tilted her head. "It looks like she'll be one of your roommates in Berry Patch Seven."

Katie was in their cabin! "Thank you!" Melanie bit her lip and grinned.

Once inside the Fireside Room, Melanie grabbed a medium-sized, midnight blue t-shirt. It had a white lighthouse on the front with the words "Light of the World" in matching white script encircling it. She retrieved a program booklet from the pile. The logo on the shirts was stamped on the cover. Placing the shirt and booklet into her backpack, Melanie went outside to join her friends as they walked back to the parking lot.

Bethany held up the shirt. "What am I going to do with this?"

"Ah, wear it," Cindy answered.

"I don't care to wear t-shirts; plus, the design is so childish." Bethany rolled her eyes. "A lighthouse. It's so quaint."

"Well, I like it," Haley said decisively. "What's with you, anyway? Can you stop acting so hoity-toity?"

"What do you mean?" Bethany narrowed her eyes.

"It's my nice way of saying—why are you acting so stuck-up?"

"She is not!" Rachel defended.

Bethany waved her off and smirked. "Daddy said you'd be jealous of me."

Haley blew out on her lips. "Yeah, sure. Keep telling yourself that. I'll see you guys later. I have to meet my parents." She stalked off.

Melanie didn't know what to do. The situation with Bethany and the rest of the girls was getting awkward. Too bad she couldn't leave with Haley. Why was Bethany making an issue out of everything, anyway? Why did she constantly have to be the center of attention? Was she going to be this annoying the whole time? It was getting old. At least, the other girls were getting tired of it, too—all except Rachel. Was this a sign of things to come? If it was, camp definitely wasn't going to be as fun as she'd hoped.

4

UNEXPECTED HELP

Back at the parking lot, some of the guys were unloading the luggage and sleeping bags from underneath the bus, one pile for each. Melanie and the other girls retrieved their stuff. Bethany and Rachel had no trouble finding guys to help them take their bags to the cabin. Trevor collected Cindy's, and Ella confidently handled her own. None of the guys offered to take Melanie's things, so she decided to wait.

Cindy volunteered, "I'll stay with you, Mel."

Melanie shook her head. "No, you go ahead. Maybe Katie will be here soon."

Other girls were waiting, too. More cars entered the parking lot. The pleasant sounds of chatter and laughter filled the air. Melanie sighed deeply, soaking in the ambience. In her heart, she knew something amazing was going to happen this week.

Melanie bit her lip out of excitement rather than nervousness. It seemed like God wanted her here. But why? She couldn't shake the feeling that there was some kind of purpose to it all. Distracted by her thoughts, Melanie didn't notice someone coming up to her.

He cleared his throat. "Do you need help?"

It was JB. "Sure." Her heart beat a little faster.

JB grabbed her suitcase with sleeping bag, and they headed toward the campgrounds.

"So, where have you been hiding?" Melanie teased boldly.

He chuckled. "I wasn't exactly hiding. Pastor Cliff and Jane needed help unloading their van for her seminar, and I volunteered. But it did help me avoid a certain someone. So, what cabin are you in?"

"I'm in Berry Patch."

JB nodded. "Those are the best cabins because they have a bathroom in them. My older sister stayed there during high school camp. Since you've never been here before, I can give you a tour on the way."

"Cool. Thanks." Why couldn't she say something more? She always felt awkward around him.

After they crossed the main bridge, Melanie noticed a carved wooden bear, which sat like a sentry against a tree. A water wheel spun next to the creek with another smaller bridge. Across from them stood a round, glass house with an encircling deck. A large sign with "Camp Redwoods" printed on it hung from the nearby redwood trees.

JB pointed up the hill to a cluster of chocolate-colored wood buildings. "Behind the round house is the tabernacle; most people call it the Tab. And that large, two-story building hidden by those trees is the gym. That's where we'll have most all of our meetings. There's also a rec room, where you can play pool, ping-pong, air hockey, and, my favorite, foosball." He grinned broadly. "Both of my parents went to camp here when they were my age. I've been coming here since I was little."

They resumed their trek along the paved path. On her right was the basketball court, which she'd noticed earlier. A circular seating area with rows and rows of benches was nestled around a fire pit to her left.

"That's the fire circle. It's where we meet before dinner. And the dining hall is upstairs." He nodded his head toward the two-story building in front of them.

Underneath the overhang of the dining hall, multiple glass doors ran the length of the walkway. It was very busy with people filing in and out. The first door they passed was the main office. A giant, painted map of the campgrounds hung on the wall outside. Next was the camp store and then the lounge.

The guys from church walked toward them. Adam snarled and brushed past her. What was wrong with him? Why was he always a jerk around her? What had she ever done? Melanie shook her head. She would avoid him as much as possible.

Melanie and JB trudged up a small hill. At a compact parking area, JB halted. In front of them was a lodge with a large sign, which read "Berry Patch."

"Here we are. I'm not allowed to go any farther."

Melanie really didn't want Bethany to see that JB had helped her, anyway, so she grabbed her suitcase handle and smiled. "Thanks, JB."

He returned her smile. "No problem."

Melanie's suitcase rattled loudly as she pulled it along the deck to Berry Patch. The cabin was on the upper level. After she rounded the corner, she passed a large window and entered the open door of number seven. Inside the room, it was refreshingly cool and clean. The walls were painted white, and so were the two sets of bunk beds flanking each side of the space. In the middle of the back wall between the beds, a door led to a bathroom. To Melanie's left was a sink with a large counter, and to her right was the entrance to another room.

Melanie took the smaller of the two lower bunks, while Cindy had one of the uppers across from her. She hung her backpack on one of the hooks and then rolled out her sleeping bag and laid out her pillow. Since she really didn't need anything else, she stored her suitcase underneath her bed.

She peeked her head into the adjoining space; it was a mirror image of their side. Haley, Ella, Rachel, and Bethany were laying out their pillows and sleeping bags in their claimed spots. Melanie sighed. Even though Bethany wasn't in her cabin, it was connected.

Rachel announced, "We need to keep our rooms neat, you know, since they judge the cleanliness of our cabins for the competition."

"Yeah," Ella said. "We want our team to win this year. Go, Green!"

"Who wants to come with me to see if Katie is here yet?" Melanie asked.

"I will." Cindy hopped down from her top bunk.

"We're coming, too." Haley and Ella scrambled out the door of their cabin onto the deck.

5

REUNITED

Back in the registration line, Melanie secretly stood behind Katie. She covered Katie's eyes and said in a sing-song voice, "Guess who?"

"Mel!" Katie squealed and turned. She hugged Melanie and then the other three girls. "Oh, Cindy, I love your hair. You look like a pixie."

Melanie elbowed Cindy and winked at her. Cindy grinned. Then she exclaimed, "Katie, you're in our cabin."

Katie squealed again.

After Katie registered, the girls returned with her to the cabin to drop off her things. As the four of them waited for Katie, Melanie perused the camp schedule.

Melanie straightened. "Cindy, there's a talent show on Wednesday night. You should sing a solo."

Cindy's eyes widened. "I'm not sure if I want to sing in front of the whole camp."

"Oh, come on," said Haley. "You know you have a beautiful voice. We've all heard it during worship time in God's Rock."

Cindy argued. "I don't have anyone to play for me."

Melanie huffed. "Excuses, excuses. I know Vivian wouldn't mind practicing and playing for you. She's your voice teacher, after all."

"I'll think about it."

Katie climbed down from her bunk above Melanie. "All right, guys. I'm ready to go." She grabbed Melanie's hand and pulled her off the bed. "Mel, I can't wait to show you everything! I just know you're going to love it here."

Melanie confessed, "I kind of got a mini-tour already."

"When did that happen?" Katie gave an over-exaggerated pout.

"When one of the guys helped me bring my stuff up from the bus," Melanie said innocently.

Cindy's forehead furrowed; then she smiled knowingly. "And who would that be? It wouldn't be JB, would it?"

Melanie smiled shyly. "Maybe."

"Shhhh!" Haley glanced to the other side of the cabin to make sure Bethany and Rachel had left. "Mermaid, you'll want to keep information like that to yourself. I know we won't tell. But if Bethany hears about it, she'll be on the rampage. So, I'd be careful if I were you."

Melanie bit her lip. She shouldn't have let that slip out. She needed to be careful around Bethany. Being here with her best friend, Katie, and her new friends, Melanie was having trouble holding back her feelings; she was too excited. Haley was right, though. She didn't want to get on Bethany's bad side. She'd already seen how cruel she could be, even with her friends.

Katie put her hands on her hips. "If you had a tour, how are we supposed to know what you've seen already?"

Melanie laughed. "I want to see it *all*, and let's start with the pool!"

Once they were outside, they crossed the camp road and climbed the steep path near their lodgings. At the top, Melanie peeked through the thick, brown slats of the fence. The pool was huge. She would swim right now if she could and skip the tour.

"When will it be open?"

Haley said, "During free time."

"Like that answer helps me. Remember, I've never gone to camp before."

"Free time is during the afternoons, Mermaid."

"So, who's coming swimming with me every day?" Melanie glanced enthusiastically at her friends.

"Every day?" Katie tried to hold back a chuckle. "But there's so much more camp has to offer. What about going canoeing with me? You know how much I love it!"

"Ahhhh! There is so much I want to do." Melanie giggled. "Camp needs to be a week longer. Okay, what's next?"

Ella raised her hand. "I vote for the gym."

"Of course, you would, El, but it's not a bad idea," Haley answered.

Balls of energy, Haley and Ella bounded down the hill with the other girls following. Instead of returning to the main area, they detoured on the road behind the buildings. After going up another small hill, the girls passed the top of the fire circle overlooking the basketball court and then the back side of the tabernacle. Another incline brought them to a massive building surrounded by tall redwood trees. Up the road, they entered through the double doors on the side entrance of the gym.

Inside, the girls showed Melanie the rec room, which was similar to the one at church with tables for pool, ping-pong, air hockey, and foosball, just like JB had said. Cute, red dispensers held balls for playing. The room also had chairs and a couple of sofas for hanging out. Upstairs, they tried to show Melanie the gym, but the door was locked.

As they exited the doors of the upper floor, Katie pointed to a trail above them. "Should we take Melanie up to the climbing tower? Ooh, and I almost forgot we should show her Treetop Village!"

Cindy made a throaty sigh. "Do we have to hike up there? It's so steep, and it's kind of hot right now."

Ella huffed. "You're beginning to sound like Bethany."

Cindy's eyes widened, and her nostrils flared. "Please never say that again." She gave a frustrated grunt. "Is it just me, or has Bethany changed? I mean, she's always been slightly snobby, especially after she visits her dad. But wasn't today a little bit over the top, even for her?" She hesitated. "Or am I being too sensitive? I mean, I mean . . ."

"Nope! You don't even need to say it," Haley insisted. "She's way over the line."

With hope in her tone, Ella said, "We should give her a couple of days; maybe she'll pop back to normal."

During the conversation, Katie and Melanie glanced at each other uncomfortably. Melanie didn't want to spend her time talking about Bethany, even if she felt the same way. Already, Bethany seemed to be ruining camp for Melanie and her friends. But she wasn't going to allow that to happen.

Melanie tilted her head with eyebrows raised. "Do I get any say in what we see next? How about somewhere where there're people?"

With pretended shock, Haley remarked, "What are we? Chopped liver?"

The girls burst out laughing.

"What? That's an expression my grandma says," she defended.

Melanie wiped her eyes. "Haley, you're too funny. And you know what I mean—I want to be where the action is."

Ella waved her arm. "We won't find it here. Everything will be pretty much deserted with everyone hanging out in the main area. Besides, I heard the guys say they were going to play basketball."

"What a surprise. Ella wants to play basketball." Haley rolled her eyes.

Katie bounced on her feet. "We should take Melanie up to the ballfield."

Haley slumped down like she was exhausted. "Even I don't want to hike up there."

"Now, who's complaining?" Cindy folded her arms and grinned.

"Is the climb really that steep? It sounds like you're being a bit overdramatic."

Haley tutted. "You'll see, Mermaid!"

Katie volunteered, "You guys go ahead. I'll show Melanie a few more spots, and we'll meet you later."

Cindy hooked her arm through Melanie's. "I'll go with you guys, too, but you're on your own if you go up to the ballfield."

6

THE FUN BEGINS

The bell rang, and they assembled at the fire circle. Bonnie enthusiastically greeted Katie, since they'd met before at Melanie's party a couple of weeks ago. Then, Katie was introduced to Bethany. Sitting on the benches, Melanie and her friends chatted. A thunderous clap drew their attention to the front, where a familiar-looking group of college-age guys stood together—it was the improv group from last year. Melanie grinned.

One of them spoke. "Hi, my name is Rafé, and we"—he waved his arm like a showman including the troupe—"are The Unscripted Hyenas." They took a bow, while the campers and counselors cheered. "It is our pleasure and privilege to be with you again this year."

Someone let out a whoop.

Rafé grinned. "Thanks. Our first skit for you this week is about the camp rules, which are listed in your program. Enjoy."

The Unscripted Hyenas were even more hilarious than they were on the videos Melanie had seen at her birthday party. Laughter echoed around the fire circle. Melanie's cheeks and stomach ached from her continuous chuckling. It was going to be an amazing week.

After their skit, Rafé prayed for the meal, and everyone moved into line to enter the dining hall above them. As they moved closer to the double doors, delectable scents wafted through the air. Melanie's mouth watered as she recognized the smell of lasagna and garlic bread. How neat that her first meal at camp happened to be her favorite.

Once inside, Melanie followed Katie along the buffet as she grabbed a tray, plate, and silverware. A server dished out a large, rectangular piece of lasagna. The cheese stretched and clung to the spatula. Using tongs, another server with a warm smile on his face placed two slices of garlic bread on her plate. Melanie politely thanked them.

She turned and exited through the gap between the partitioned walls. The enormous dining hall had a grand, wood-beamed ceiling. Round tables with attached benches were placed in neat rows separated by another buffet. Long tables ran underneath the windows. Before finding a seat, Melanie retrieved a drink and then helped herself to the salad bar.

All eight of them from their cabin sat together at one of the round tables with Cindy and Katie on either side of her. Melanie took a bite of her lasagna. It was the perfect blend of cheese, red sauce, and noodles—just the way she liked it.

Cindy inquired, "So what do you think of the camp food, Mel?"

"It's delicious. Why in the world did I get salad when I already want seconds of this?" Using her fork, she pointed to her food and licked her lips.

"Ugh!" Bethany interjected. "Seconds on this greasy food? What about your complexion?"

Melanie raised her eyebrows and shrugged. "I haven't thought about it."

"If you want to get a boy's attention, you really should start to care," Bethany informed her.

Cindy tilted her head. "I don't think Melanie is going to have trouble with that. Someone already likes her."

"Really? Who?" Bethany leaned forward.

As Melanie hit Cindy's leg underneath the table, she sputtered out the first name that popped into her head. "Adam." Melanie saw Katie shake her head.

Bethany pursed her lips. "Don't be silly. Adam likes me, though I'd never give him the time of day. He's so pathetic."

"He is not!" Ella defended.

Bethany rolled her eyes and sighed loudly. "Anyway, my dad took me . . ."

Melanie tuned her out. She didn't want to hear any more bragging from Bethany. But hopefully, Bethany would be too absorbed in herself to realize Melanie had fibbed about Adam, and it was actually JB that Cindy had been talking about. Did JB really like her in that way, or was he just being nice? Cindy seemed to think he liked her. But maybe she was wrong.

After dinner, the girls headed to the cabin to retrieve their Bibles, programs, and jackets. Cindy sprayed herself with bug repellent. She offered it to the girls, who accepted. Then it was back to the gym for Tab Time to hear the evening message. Bethany and Rachel stayed behind fixing their hair and refreshing their make-up.

Melanie asked, "Katie, why do we call it Tab Time, since we meet in the gym?"

Katie responded, "I hadn't thought of that. It's always been Tab Time because we used to meet in the tabernacle. But camp has grown so large, now we're in the gym." She shrugged.

Melanie tilted her head. "I guess if they called it gym time, people would think we'd be exercising."

Katie and Melanie snickered.

As they entered the double doors of the gymnasium, Bonnie waved them over to the second row. Melanie sat down and looked around. It was a typical gym but without bleachers, and there was also a climbing wall roped off in the back corner. The guys from their church were sitting behind them. JB smiled at her. Melanie smiled in return but quickly turned her head back toward the front before he could notice she was blushing.

A young guy wearing a backward baseball cap went up to the front. "Greetings, Campers! I'm Nelson, and I'm in charge of rec this week. Our first game is tonight!"

Cheers rang out.

Nelson beamed. "So, after Tab tonight, grab your flashlights and dress warmly. When the bell rings, meet in the tabernacle."

Nelson announced the worship band, Anticipate, a husband and wife duo. The wife, Livi, played the guitar and lead vocals, and her husband, Xavier, played the keyboard. Since attending youth group the last few weeks, Melanie was familiar with some of the music. While they were singing, Bethany and Rachel finally joined them at the end of the row. After they sang a few songs, Livi introduced the speaker.

A medium-sized man with a black mustache came up front and placed his Bible on the podium. Grinning broadly at them, he spoke into the microphone. "Hi. Like Livi said, my name is Eddie Jay, and I'll be your speaker this week. I feel blessed to be teaching all of you here at camp. When I was asked to speak, they told me the theme would be 'Light of the World.' I've been pondering that phrase and praying about what God would want me to share with you. He gave me this cool idea for a demonstration." He nodded to someone in the back.

The lights turned off, startling a few of the kids. The room was completely black. Then there was a click, and a flashlight beamed out into the darkness held by Eddie Jay. He focused the light on his Bible and read, "John 8:12. 'Then Jesus again spoke to them, saying, *I am the Light of the world; the one who follows Me will not walk in the darkness, but will have the Light of life.'*"

Then he repeated the verse. He nodded again, and the lights turned on.

"Jesus is the Light of the world. What does that mean? This world isn't dark. We have the sun to light the day and the moon to shine at night." He paused. "But Jesus wasn't talking about physical darkness; He's talking about spiritual darkness, which all started with Adam and Eve and their sin in the garden. Sin brought darkness and death to this world. But God defeated darkness by sending His Son, Jesus, to die for us and cover our sin by the shedding of His blood."

Tears formed in his eyes, and his voice cracked with emotion. "He became our Light in the darkness of this world. Jesus left Heaven because He loved us so much. And He loves us today! Even in our sin, He loves us and wants us to live with Him forever. The only way to do that was to sacrifice Himself."

Eddie Jay explained why Jesus had to come and die for everyone. Melanie had heard some of this before in youth group and in her Sunday school class. Even Katie had tried to explain it to her. So, the idea wasn't new to her, but for some reason, she still didn't quite understand it. God had been showing her He loved and cared for her this summer already. But God dying on the cross for people thousands of years ago? It was so hard to believe. Her heart thumped softly in her chest.

Melanie continued to listen to Eddie Jay as he shared about God's love and the light of Jesus. There was something about the man; he was so heartfelt and authentic. And the way he spoke, it was obvious he loved God and believed every word he said. He was so confident in his belief, his excitement was infectious. His words captivated her and drew in Melanie. Could she really have a relationship with God like that?

All too soon, it was over. Eddie Jay ended in prayer. When he had finished, he gleefully said, "Tomorrow we'll be talking about how we can become lights to the world like Christ is." He waved them out. "Guys, have fun tonight at rec!"

7

NIGHT GAME

They took their Bibles and programs back to the cabin. Melanie and the others retrieved their flashlights. Out on the deck, Cindy doused herself and anyone else who wanted it with another layer of bug repellent. The bell rang, and they hurried to the tabernacle, leaving behind Bethany and Rachel. It was finally rec time. Her friends had been talking about it for weeks.

In the tabernacle, the girls looked around for Bonnie, but they couldn't find her. Pastor Brett wasn't there either. Strangely, Jane was the only counselor, and she was laying across some chairs with her leg propped up on a cushion.

Alarmed, Haley rushed over to her mother. "Mom, are you hurt?"

"I'm fine, sweetie."

"What happened?"

Jane waved her hand. "Nothing."

"Okay." Haley's voice crackled with worry.

Cindy interjected, "Where are all the counselors?"

Jane smiled. "You'll find out."

At that moment, Nelson sprang up onto the stage and practically shouted into the microphone, "Hey, Campers!"

Startled, a few people jumped, including Melanie. Several snickers escaped the quieting crowd.

"Welcome to our first rec game of the week! Who's up for a game of hide-and-seek?"

Someone yelled, "Woo-hoo!"

Nelson saluted them and continued, "In this game of hide-and-seek, you will need to find the counselors. Each counselor is worth points, and there are three counselors who are worth bonus points. When you find a counselor, you must tag them and say your name and team color." After explaining the rest of the rules, Nelson dismissed them. When the girls exited the tabernacle, Bethany and Rachel arrived. Rachel had changed into warmer clothes, but Bethany had just refreshed her hair and make-up and was still wearing her high-heeled boots. Neither of them had a flashlight.

Haley looked at Bethany's outfit and pursed her lips. "So, you're going hiking in those ritzy clothes and boots?"

Bethany shrugged. "How was I supposed to know we'd be hiking?"

Ella gave an exasperated sigh. "It's called rec. What did you think we would be doing? Painting our nails or something?"

"I don't have to play. I can stay here in the tabernacle and keep warm."

"Nope," Ella responded. "You're coming with us. Per the rules, we need to go out as a cabin. You'd know that if you'd been here on time."

"I don't see what the big deal is."

Cindy seethed. "The big deal is you're late. We're trying to have fun, and you keep making things difficult."

Bethany daintily laid her hand on her chest, and her eyes grew wide. "Me? What did I do?"

Ella growled. "We're wasting time."

Katie suggested, "We should look near the bridge down by the creek."

They strode down the hill to the main area. Around them, shadowy figures of other teams waved their flashlight beams, searching the campgrounds. It reminded Melanie of Eddie Jay's demonstration of light shining in the darkness. As they reached the lower main area, they bumped into two other groups who had the same idea.

Ella stopped, and the girls gathered around her. "It looks like we're too late. Maybe we should go up to the ballfield instead. I bet one of those extra point counselors has hidden up there."

Bethany started to grumble, but Ella shot her an angry glare.

"You're probably right, Ella," Katie said. "But I think we'll run into the same problem. We should've tried there first."

"I can't believe I'm going to suggest this," said Cindy, "but the most likely place for a counselor to be hidden would be around the climbing tower."

"But I can't walk up that trail in these shoes," Bethany whined.

"Whose fault is that?" Haley shook her head.

The girls tramped back up the hill toward the tabernacle. The light from the windows cast an inviting glow into the night. The evening air kissed Melanie's cheeks with its chill. She shivered, but she couldn't tell if it was from the cold or from exploring in the dark—maybe a little of both. Along the road, another group approached them.

It was the guys from their youth group. Melanie still didn't know everyone's names, expect JB, Adam, and the most recent boy she'd met, Cam. Since Cam wore glasses, he reminded Melanie of her dad. The boys put the beam of their flashlights in their own faces and made ghoulish noises. Bethany squealed and cowered conveniently close to JB.

One of them demanded, "Where are you guys going?"

Ella muttered, "Why would we tell you?"

"We're on the same team."

She gave an exasperated sigh. "Then, wouldn't it be better if we spread out more to cover more ground?"

Cam dodged his head back and forth. "Wow, so strategic. We thought you'd want us around to keep you safe from the snipes."

"Snipes!" Bethany wailed. "What are snipes?"

Melanie had never heard of them either. Scrunching her shoulders, she held her hands to her chest as Cam described the large, rodent-like creatures with sharp teeth strong enough to drag someone into the woods. From what he said, it was better if they were in groups. And if you were alone at night, you should tap two sticks together loudly to scare them away.

The more Cam explained, the more anxious Melanie became. Why hadn't her parents warned her about snipes? She would need to be more careful at night, even in her own backyard. If there were snipes around camp, they must live close to her house, too. Melanie bit her lip.

Katie grabbed her arm and whispered in her ear, "Snipes aren't real."

Bethany reacted like she was more frightened by the minute. Grasping JB's arm, she leaned into him. "I'm scared. Will you protect me?"

Haley growled loudly. "You guys, there's no such thing as snipes! Maybe you've forgotten, but you tried pranking us with that last year. Ugh, at least get some new material."

Cam crossed his arms. "Ah, Haley, why'd ya have to ruin it? We had Bethany going there."

Ella sighed and waved them over. "Come on, girls. Let's just ignore these guys and get back to the game." She climbed up the trail with Haley following. Katie, Cindy, and Melanie raced to catch up.

Cindy turned around. "Rachel!"

Bethany peeped out, "What about me? You aren't going to leave me, are you? What about the rules?"

"No, Bethany, but hurry up."

Bethany scampered up the hill, surprisingly abandoning the guys. Cindy waited for her and Rachel. The three of them trailed behind Melanie and Katie. But before they reached the climbing tower, another group strutted down toward them with a counselor. They were too late again. Disappointed, the girls returned and used the remainder of their time poking around closer to the tabernacle.

The warning bell sounded, and the girls entered the tabernacle cold and disheartened. Thankfully, some of the other kids on their team had found a couple of counselors, so the green team wasn't doing too badly. But according to the white board with the scores, one of the counselors who was worth the most hadn't been found yet. The girls stood near Jane with her leg propped up and also Bonnie, who'd been located by another team. As more and more kids and counselors entered the tab, the noise level grew.

Katie tilted her blonde head and then grinned widely. "I think I've got it." She put her hand on Jane's shoulder and said, "I've found you. Katie from the green team."

Jane jumped up, hollering. She waved excitedly to Nelson and yelled, "The green team."

Haley's eyes widened. "Mom! Your leg?"

Jane shimmied over to her daughter. "Gotcha! There's nothing wrong with my leg. If you remember, I told you I was fine."

With Katie's last minute discovery, the green team placed first. The girls and guys on their team congratulated her. After the game, everyone returned to their cabins for lights out. Melanie hurriedly changed into her pajamas and snuggled into her warm sleeping bag.

Before Bonnie turned off the light, she asked, "Does anyone want to go to morning worship with me?"

The girls remained silent.

Bonnie laughed. "I didn't want to get up early when I was your age either. Well, the invitation is open all week. Good night, girls."

"Good night," they answered.

Melanie closed her eyes. What a wonderful day. Her first day at camp was everything she'd thought it would be and more. *Thank You, God.* Melanie smiled and fell asleep.

8

SOULO TIME & REC

After a delicious breakfast of French toast, hash browns, and sausage, Melanie and her friends waited patiently in the gym for Tab Time to begin. She perused the program for their next activity. It was Soulo Time. What was that?

Melanie pointed to the schedule on her booklet and asked Katie. "What is this Soulo Time? Did they spell it wrong? It's got an added 'u.'"

Katie's eyes twinkled. "No, it's a play on words. During Soulo Time, we are supposed to find a place where we are alone or *solo* and spend time with God working on our *souls*. Get it?"

Melanie tilted her head. "Actually, that's pretty clever."

Finding the page in her own program, Katie showed Melanie. "See, these are the questions we need to read and answer during Soulo Time. Just do the best you can. Afterward, we'll discuss them as a cabin."

Melanie made a sly smile. "It doesn't take a genius, Katie, to know where you'll be having your Soulo Time."

Katie beamed. "Yep, it'll be in my favorite spot by the creek, as long as I can get there first." She put her index finger to the corner of her lips. "And I'm sure I can guess where you'll be."

Melanie's eyes widened. "Oh! You're right. I should sit by the pool."

"It won't be open yet, but you can sit on the bench outside."

During Soulo Time, Melanie leaned her back against the pool fence. The familiar scent of chlorine beckoned to her, but she would have to wait until free time to swim. If only the gate wasn't locked, she could stick her feet into the crystal, clear water. She sighed.

Sunlight warmed her shoulders as Melanie opened the pamphlet to look over the questions for Soulo Time. With her new Bible on her lap, Melanie paged to the Table of Contents to find the verses she needed to read. After she had finished a few of the questions, the camp janitor began cleaning the nearby bathroom. The rattle of his bucket's wheels and the sloshing of his mop interrupted the quietness. Then, he began to sing in Spanish.

His sweet voice echoed off the tiled walls, creating an acoustical symphony. She understood only a few of the words, but the ones that rang out resounded like love notes to God. The depth of his feelings poured out in his heartfelt praise and worship. It was so beautiful.

Closing her eyes, the music washed over her. She basked in the wonder of the moment. Her heart thumped and pulsed a rhythm. *God, You've shown me You love and care for me. But I still don't understand what You want from me. I feel like You're calling me, but I don't know how to answer.* Peace settled over her as the melody became familiar. She recognized it as one of the songs from Anticipate's worship sets.

"La luz del mundo es Jesús," the man trilled.

Melanie began to sing along with him in English. "The Light of the world is Jesus." Humming the tune, she continued to harmonize with him on the parts she knew.

The bell clanged loudly, disrupting the sacred moment. Melanie wiped a tear from her cheek as she reluctantly gathered her things. She joined her cabinmates on the benches across from their lodge.

During the cabin discussion, Melanie tried to listen, but her thoughts kept wandering back to Soulo Time. How could someone be so happy scrubbing toilets? The janitor had such an ordinary job, yet he praised God. Joy had flowed from him. What had made him feel that way?

When they finished their discussion, the girls dropped off their stuff, since it was time for rec. All the teams were to meet at the ballfield. They rushed to the other side of the campground. At the back end of the parking lot, hidden behind the trees, a wide bridge spanned over the creek. A sign marked the path.

As they rounded the bend in the road, Bethany groaned as they strode up the steep incline. "Ugh! Why can't someone drive us up to the ballfield?"

Ella turned around, walking backward. "It's not that bad."

Cindy blew out her tongue. "Easy for you to say."

Melanie agreed with Bethany and the others. Her shins burned as she climbed. After a few minutes, the road leveled off, but the path up to the ballfield continued on.

Haley stopped, then pointed above them to round structures nestled on the side of the forested hill. "Check it out, Mermaid."

Melanie halted. "Are those yurts?" She'd seen similar tent-like dwellings on a TV show.

"Yep," Haley answered. "I wish you could see the inside, but the staff stay there."

Bonnie motioned for them to catch up. They followed her around the curve to the base of a monumental slope.

Melanie's eyes widened. "If I knew I would be scaling Everest, I would have brought mountain gear."

Bonnie and Haley laughed.

When they reached the summit, the trees thinned and opened up into an amphitheater with tiers of benches. Campers and counselors congregated in groups. Four enormous earth balls leaned against a tall chain-link fence, which bordered the grassy area. A thick wire hung from the top of a platform on the upper hillside to a tree on the opposite side of the field.

Katie ran over and dragged her toward their team. Bonnie joined Pastor Brett, and Haley stood near her parents. Melanie pursed her lips when she saw Bethany close to JB. But judging from the perturbed expression on his face, JB wasn't happy with the situation either.

Nelson's voice squawked through the megaphone as he stood on the deck above them. Melanie couldn't understand him because of the enthusiastic noise around her. Jane's screeching whistle silenced everyone.

"Thank you," Nelson said. "All right! Who wants to play some games?"

They cheered, jumping with excitement.

First, Nelson lined them up as a team. Each team member stood behind the other. One of his assistants gave each team a hula hoop. The object of the game was to get the hula hoop through the entire line of bodies. When it was her turn, Melanie dropped the hula hoop over her head and leaped over it.

Next was tug-of-war. After two rounds, their guy's team ended up coming in second. Then it was the girls' turn. Melanie and seven other girls took their place on the rope. With all her swimming, Melanie was one of the more athletic ones on their team. With her height and muscular frame, Ella was their strongest girl, so they made her the anchor. Bethany got into position in front of Melanie.

Tightening her grip on the rough, coiled rope, Melanie leaned back and braced herself. When Nelson signaled, Melanie tugged as hard as she could. The rope became taut. Melanie bent her legs and dug her heels into the grass. The team gained ground as

Ella pulled them backward. The other team lost their footing, and Melanie's team won.

Their final match was against the blue team, which had a few bigger girls. The sun beat down on the field. Melanie wiped her sweaty hands on her shorts and then grabbed the rope. Ready in her stance, she waited anxiously for the game to begin.

Nelson signaled, and Melanie strained against the resistance of the cord. She planted her feet in the tufts of sod and drew back. One of the girls in front faltered, but their team held on. Inch by inch, they recovered. With a quick, hard yank from their side, it was over. The green team had won.

Uproarious cheering erupted from their team. Melanie and the other girls jumped up and down and high-fived each other. Even Bethany couldn't contain her excitement and hugged Melanie. But the friendliness was short-lived when JB grinned and gave Melanie a thumbs up.

The next game was earth ball soccer. All four teams were on the field at once with two earth balls on the loose. With her teammates, Melanie tried to push one of the gigantic balls into another team's goal. Succeeding in their efforts, the game started again. Unfortunately, Rachel was toppled over and ended up resting on the sidelines until the game was over.

Taking a break, Melanie sat with Rachel as they watched the chariot races ensue. Representing their team, Haley balanced a large ball, while her parents carried her across the field. When they won, Melanie and Rachel cheered along with their team.

Gazing up at the thick wire overhead, she pointed and asked Rachel, "What is that for?"

Rachel brushed aside her long, brown bangs from her eyes. "Oh, that's the Flying Squirrel. See the platform at the top of the benches? Up there, they attach a seat to the wire, strap you in, and let you fly."

"Um, but how do you get off?"

Rachel laughed. "That's the scary part. When the seat stops, it hangs in the middle of the field. They have a rope attached to the bottom of the seat, and they pull it down. You have to jump off."

Melanie's eyes widened. "That's so cool. I'm glad I'm here. This place is amazing."

9

FREE TIME

At free time, Melanie, Katie, and Cindy walked up the hill with their beach towels slung over their shoulders. When Melanie entered the gate, she noticed JB, Adam, and Cam horsing around in the pool. Bethany lounged on the edge dangling her feet in the water, laughing at something Cam said. Rachel giggled next to her.

Reclining on the other side of the deck, Haley waved them over. The girls unfurled their towels, laid them down in a row, and then coated themselves with sunblock. While her friends proceeded to the shallow area, Melanie took the opportunity to get in some real swim time. Standing on the coping at the deep end, Melanie grinned at the sparkling blue expanse. With arms flat against her sides, she plunged in feet first. The cool water washed over her. When she touched the bottom, she pushed herself up. As she rose to the surface, she blew out air bubbles through her nose.

She touched the wall and then began to swim a lap across the width of the pool. Melanie concentrated on her breaststroke technique. Pull, breathe, kick, glide. When she grabbed the side for a break, JB swam up beside her.

"Are you having fun?" he asked.

Melanie raised her eyebrows. "Of course, I am. I'm swimming."

JB grinned. "No, I meant here at camp?"

"Oh, yes. I'm having the best time ever." Why couldn't she say something clever? When she was around JB, she became flustered and tongue-tied. His freckled face was so adorable; plus, he was so sweet. Behind JB, Melanie's gaze lifted to Bethany, who was glaring at them.

JB heaved a sigh. "Is she watching us?"

Melanie nodded.

"I wish she'd listen. I already told her I made a promise to God I wouldn't date until I'm older." JB grabbed the rung of the ladder. "Even if I like someone now." He climbed out.

Melanie's heart raced, and she bit her lip. Did that mean JB liked her, too? But from what he said, he wasn't into dating. Maybe that's what his promise ring meant.

She'd been wondering about that. She glanced up. Bethany was still glowering. Ignoring Bethany, Melanie coursed through the water for a couple more laps. It was a relief to be back in her favorite environment. Sometimes, she really felt like a real-life mermaid.

Because of her family's recent circumstances, she'd given up swimming to ease the burden on her parents to take her to the pool center. Her mom should be healed by the time swim season began; she could hardly wait to be on a team again. Hopefully, she would be the fastest in the breaststroke. When she finished practicing, Melanie swam over to the other side of the pool to be with her friends, passing Adam and Cam, who were throwing a ball to each other.

Katie sat on the pool steps, since she didn't care for swimming. Cindy and Haley stood near her in the shallow area. Bethany and Rachel had moved over closer to them. The girls were laughing together. Cindy waved her arms as she spoke.

Within earshot, Melanie listened as Cindy shared, "You guys, during Soulo Time, I realized . . . well, I feel like I should sing in the talent show."

"Wahoo! You're going to be so good." Haley clapped.

Cindy smiled. "Thanks for the vote of confidence." Her eyes grew large. "I hope I don't mess it up."

"You'll be amazing," Katie encouraged. "Great experience for when you become a professional singer."

Grinning even wider, Cindy prattled on, detailing her plans for the song, arranging practice time with Vivian, and thinking aloud about what she might wear.

Bethany sighed heavily. "Cindy, do you ever stop talking? I'm trying to relax and get a little sun."

Cindy's face reddened, and she shut her mouth.

Haley bit out, "Excuse you! Our friend was talking. You don't need to be rude. If it bothers you, move over to the deck. Go ahead, Cin."

"No, that's okay," Cindy mumbled.

Bethany tilted her head, put on a dazzling smile, and said, "Oh, Adam."

Adam turned around with the ball in his hand and gave Bethany his full attention. He seemed practically star-struck.

"Melanie thinks you like her," Bethany announced.

Color drained from Melanie's face.

Adam snarled, "No, I don't. Why would I be interested in a scrawny thing like her? She's not even pretty."

Melanie bit her lip. Why did he need to be so cruel? So, Adam didn't like her; but he didn't have to insult her, too. But all that didn't matter if JB had heard. When she looked, he was talking to some guys with his back turned. Good, probably not. Would he find out, though? And what would he think? Oh, why did she have to accidentally lie and say she thought Adam liked her? What a mess.

Pushing the incident aside, Melanie goofed around with her friends. A ball sailed near them, splashing Cindy. In turn, she lobbed the ball to Cam, purposely spraying him. Then it was an all-out war, the girls against the guys. Water flew in all directions. Adam created a tremendous wave, which drenched Bethany.

She shrilled, shaking herself off. "I'm soaked!"

Cam chuckled. "That happens when you're around a pool."

Bethany strutted off in a huff. "Rachel, I need my towel."

The water fight continued with the girls squealing and laughing. The guys tried their best, but it was four against two in the girls' favor. Without warning, hands clamped down on Melanie's shoulders and dunked her. She barely had time to catch a breath. Her legs swept out from under her. When she regained her footing, Melanie tried to wiggle out of the person's grasp. But they were too strong for her.

Pulling on their wrists, she fought back, trying to loosen their grip. Melanie's heart raced, and her chest burned. Finally, the perpetrator released her, and she burst above the surface. Melanie gasped for air and filled her lungs. Coughing and sputtering, she wiped the water from her eyes and face.

Cindy rushed over to her. "What is wrong with you, Adam?"

"That's what she gets for spreading lies about me." He shrugged. "What's the big deal? I held her down for only a few seconds."

Glaring, Cindy angrily shouted, "That was longer than a few seconds!"

"Dude, that was not cool." Cam sloshed through the water. "Are you okay, Mel?"

She nodded as she waded over to the pool steps.

Adam waved his hand dismissively. "See? She's fine."

Melanie hurriedly grabbed her towel and exited the gate. Tears threatened. Biting her lip, she grunted. No, she was not going to cry because of Adam and Bethany. Sure, that had been terrifying, but she wasn't going to let them get to her. With determination, she walked down to her cabin. After showering and dressing, Melanie washed out her bathing suit and hung it on the railing to dry. Hopefully, nothing else would go wrong.

10

TAB TIME

In the evening, they sat waiting for Tab Time to begin. The lights dimmed. On the wall, a slide show projected the day's events. Katie elbowed her when Melanie popped up in a photo of her and Ella during tug-of-war. Melanie then returned the action when Katie's face appeared in another shot. Quite a few were of Bethany with her hand on her hip, posing for the camera with her model-like smile. Melanie frowned and shook her head. What a show-off.

After the lights returned to normal, Nelson announced the team standings for rec. Green was in second. The girls cheered. When he mentioned The Unscripted Hyenas would be performing for them tonight after Tab, they hollered even louder.

Next, Anticipate led them in worship. Melanie's heart thumped a rhythm when they sang, "The Light of the World Is Jesus." She smiled, remembering the janitor singing the same song earlier in the day. Like usual, Cindy belted out the words. Joy exuded from her face. What would it be like to feel that way, too?

Before they could sit down, Eddie Jay waved for them to keep standing as he grabbed the microphone. "Evenin', guys! I have another illustration for you tonight, but I need your participation." He held up his hand and pointed with his index finger to the sky. "Can anyone guess what this symbolizes?"

Someone yelled out, "Number one."

"Good, good, but I'm looking for something different. Anyone else? It has to do with our camp theme."

"'This Little Light of Mine,'" another answered.

"Bingo!" Eddie Jay exclaimed. "And we're going to sing it together. Now, get your lights ready and don't be shy."

Katie flicked her thumb against her index finger like she was lighting a match, igniting her pretend candle. Playfully, she touched Melanie's upright finger as though she lit it with her own. As they sang, Melanie learned the song easily with its repeating lyrics. The girls exaggerated the motions and words of the verses. Pastor Brett joined them in their enthusiastic antics. When it was over, they plopped down in their seats.

Eddie Jay asked them to open their Bibles to Matthew 5:14-16. Katie helped Melanie find the passage. When the room quieted, he read, "'You are the light of the world. A city set on a hill cannot be hidden; nor do *people* light a lamp and put it under a basket, but on the lampstand, and it gives light to all who are in the house. Your light must shine before people in such a way that they may see your good works, and glorify your Father who is in heaven.'"

He echoed, "'You are the light of the world.'" Rubbing his hands together, Eddie Jay explained, "I love this part! Do you know why? It's another instance in our Christian life where we experience a partnership with God. We know this from the book of John when Jesus calls Himself, 'the Light of the world.' Our Savior lives inside us, where His light shines out to others. Isn't our God wonderful, coming into these broken bodies and into our hearts to dwell within us?"

Even though Melanie didn't understand all the things Eddie Jay said about God, the sincerity of his words compelled her to want to know more. Jesus wanted to live inside her? How could He do that? They'd mentioned something similar in church a few times, so it must be true. But what did it mean?

"Our thoughtful and caring actions," Eddie Jay continued, "shine brightly for others to see the Light of Jesus. What have you done to shine the Light for others? Is there any person you've touched or reached out to, to express the love of Jesus?"

Melanie's heart skipped a beat, and she swallowed hard, biting her lip. She was that person. Most of her friends had mentioned at one time or another they'd been praying for her. And when her mother had gotten hurt, the church had rallied around them, providing help and food, even raising money for her to be here. All their kindness came rushing to her mind. She wiped a tear from her eye.

After Tab Time, the girls dropped off their stuff in the cabin and grabbed a snack in the dining hall. Then they headed over to the tabernacle with the rest of the campers for The Unscripted Hyenas' comedy set. As they performed, Melanie's body rocked with chuckles. How could they be so funny?

For their next act, The Unscripted Hyenas sauntered on stage wearing cowboy hats and boots. Rafé sat down like he was warming his hands by a campfire. The other troupe members paused, waiting for him. When he spoke, the cast mimed the actions of his story.

"Howdy, folks. I'm a goin' to tell ya' all the story 'bout Slingshot David and the Outlaw Goliath. It's not a tall tale like some old cowpokes jaw 'round campfires. It's God's honest truth. I heared the story froms a feller be a Samuel. It's a story about the Ol' West. The real Ol' West so far away, some call it East. A town be of the name of Israel. Now, Israel be full up with decent folks, God-fearin' people.

"One day, a gang of outlaws came a-ridin' into Israel. Their name bein' the Philistine Gang. And the leader o' this gang be a man named Goliath. He bein' a giant o' a man. They say he be nine feet tall."

When their show was over, the campers gave them a standing ovation and yelled for an encore. The Unscripted Hyenas obliged with one more skit. It was late when the girls returned to their cabin. With her cheeks and stomach sore from laughter, Melanie burrowed into her sleeping bag. Sighing, she fell asleep quickly after her first full day of camp.

SWIM GAMES

After the morning's cabin discussions, Melanie walked along the lodge's deck. She scanned for her bathing suit, which she'd left outside. The other girls' suits were there, but she didn't see hers. That was strange. Melanie riffled through them. Her swimsuit was missing! Had it fallen? Leaning over the rail, she peered below. No navy blue material popped out, but she needed to make sure.

On the ground level, Melanie searched the walkway and the surrounding greenery. Maybe it was hidden in one of the large bushes. She sifted through them, but she didn't find it. Melanie's chest grew heavy. She pulled in a deep breath, trying to keep the tears away. *Not this, too. Not now!*

"Melanie," Bonnie called from above, "what are you doing?"

"I left my bathing suit to dry on the railing yesterday. It's gone." Her voice wobbled. "I thought it may have dropped down here."

"Maybe one of the girls brought it in. I'll check." She went back inside the cabin.

Why didn't she think of that first? Maybe someone took hers in by mistake. That's probably what had happened. Melanie ran up the stairs.

In the cabin, Bonnie helped Melanie search. "I'm sorry; it doesn't look like it's here. But it could be in this mess somewhere." She motioned to Melanie's clothes scattered around the room. "Maybe you could borrow someone's."

Katie grabbed her towel. "Mel, I can't believe you didn't bring a spare or two."

Melanie's eyes widened. "I did! I completely forgot." Rustling through her suitcase, she grabbed one and raced into the bathroom.

Up at the pool, campers and counselors from both the red and green teams swarmed the deck area. Weaving their way through the throng, the girls found an open space where they could stand together and watch the competition. Floating in the middle of the pool, an enormous pile of black inner tubes was tied together in the shape of a pyramid. Hanging from a wire at the top of the giant structure was an upside-down rubber chicken. The toy swayed from side to side. What kind of crazy games did they have planned for them?

Haley clapped enthusiastically. "With the mermaid on our team, we're sure to win."

Melanie bit her lip. Normally, she would've been confident with her swimming ability but not after the drama with Adam yesterday and her missing swimsuit. A shiver traveled along her back when she gazed at the churning waters. Her pulse pounded. Why couldn't she shake this feeling?

Katie nudged her and whispered in her ear, "Are you okay?"

"Not really."

"You don't have to do this."

"If I don't, Adam will bully me, since everyone's been telling him what a good swimmer I am."

"You are a great swimmer. Nothing will change that." Then Katie teased, "I could take your place."

Melanie guffawed. "Don't be silly. I don't even know if I'd call what you do swimming; you can barely dog paddle."

Katie placed her hands on her hips. "Fine! I offered. I guess it's up to you."

Melanie bit her lip with a small smile. How did Katie do that? She sensed Melanie's doubts and tried to encourage her. What a friend. Melanie wouldn't let her team down.

Roger, another rec leader, was in charge of the pool games. Using his megaphone, he quieted them down and explained the first challenge. Each team would need three boys, three girls, one female counselor, and one male counselor. The object of the relay was for each person to dive in, swim to the pyramid, climb it, touch the chicken, and swim back.

Melanie, JB, Adam, and a few others from the green team volunteered; and the counselors, Pastor Brett, and Jane organized them into a line. Since Melanie and JB were the fastest swimmers, she was placed second-to-last with JB following her. When the whistle blew, Pastor Brett and the guy from the red team plunged in first.

Both competitors struggled to ascend the teetering stack of inner tubes. When Pastor Brett was close enough to slap at the chicken, his foot slipped, and he plummeted into the water. Adam clenched his fists and grunted loudly. While Pastor Brett struggled back up, the red team moved ahead.

When it was Jane's turn, Haley stood by her dad as they rooted for her. Next, Adam clambered up the pyramid with difficulty. After slipping a couple of times, he finally succeeded in whacking the rubber chicken. Then he tumbled into the water, rocking the unstable buoys. The girl from the opposing team lost her balance and fell into the pool.

As Melanie continued to watch the competition, her unease grew. The diving and swimming would be easy, but everyone wrestled with the inner tubes. How was she going to get to the top? What if she couldn't climb up and caused her team to lose? If that happened, how much more intolerable would Adam become since her friends had bragged about her?

Waiting for her turn, Melanie readied herself in her stance and curled her toes around the edge of the coping. It was a tight race, and their team was behind. Melanie blocked out the sound of the crowd and concentrated on doing her best. As her teammate touched the wall, Melanie dove in.

The cool water and the familiarity of her strokes energized her. When Melanie reached the pyramid, she grabbed one of the slick, black inner tubes, but her hand slipped off. Instead of trying again, Melanie wrapped her arm around the tire and pulled herself up. It worked. Gritting her teeth, she carefully but quickly scaled one of the sides while straining to keep her balance.

Close to the top, Melanie leaned against the upper rows. Extending her arm, she slammed the chicken, and it bobbled in the air. Yay! She got it. Melanie turned, jumped into the water, and swam back as fast as she could.

"Great job!" a girl said as she helped Melanie out of the pool and handed her a towel.

Melanie dried off her face and then spun around. She didn't want to miss the last part of the relay. In the time she'd gotten out, JB had begun climbing the pyramid, and so had the other guy who was the last remaining member from the red team. They scrambled up the sides. The race was so close. Both of them hit the chicken and dove back in. JB pulled slightly ahead. When he contacted the wall, their team roared. They had won!

Everyone was congratulating each other with high-fives and fist bumps. Melanie sighed with relief. She hadn't made a fool of herself. JB and Adam came toward her.

Adam nodded. "Not bad, Fishface."

JB folded his arms across his chest. "Hey, dude, show some respect. Melanie caught up to the other team and then gave us the lead."

"Ahh, whatever." Adam dismissed them with a wave of his hand.

"Wow, Mel. You are fast! No wonder you're nicknamed Mermaid. Adam won't admit it, but you won the game for us."

Then Roger began explaining the second game. Each team was to prevent the other from touching the chicken. Only the campers were allowed to participate. The green team would be on defense in the water for the first part. Melanie, JB, and another guy from their team, Lewis, were grouped together to guard the pyramid from the deep end.

After the signal sounded, most of the action happened in the shallow area. As Melanie treaded water, one of the guys from the other team swam to their side. He pulled himself up quickly as Melanie swam over. She grabbed his ankle, and he kicked to loosen her grip. With extreme effort, Melanie held on until Roger blew the whistle.

Too tired to participate in the second half, Melanie shouted encouragement from the sidelines with Katie, Cindy, and Haley. On offense, Adam aggressively earned the first point for their team. Practically unstoppable, Ella scaled the inner tubes and struck the chicken right after him. Others from their team scored. When the game ended, they'd trounced the red team.

Wrapped in her towel, Melanie rested on the planter wall during the last event: the belly-flop contest. Quite a few campers and even a couple of counselors lined up to undertake the ambitious feat. Pastor Brett was the first one to attempt it. He did a near-perfect belly-flop with his arms and legs spread out. When his body hit the water, a loud slap echoed across the swim area. Melanie cringed. It was impressive, but it must've hurt.

Ever the showoff, Adam strutted up for his turn. Yelling like a caveman, he threw himself into the deep end. His belly-flop created plenty of splash but not a lot of sound. Adam exited the pool near them.

Ella tilted her head and with a teasing smirk said to him, "Ehh, I'd give you maybe a six. That's being generous."

"Hey! What?" he complained. "That was definitely at least an eight." He rubbed his chest. "But it hurt more like a ten." He playfully punched Ella's arm.

Why hadn't she noticed before that Ella and Adam were friends? And why was Ella so nice to someone like him? Maybe she didn't realize how cruel he was. She hadn't been there yesterday, but then again, that hadn't been the first time Adam had been mean to her. Melanie shook her head. It was a mystery.

12

TIME FLIES WHEN YOU'RE HAVING FUN

Reddish-brown pine needles blanketed the rugged dirt path as Melanie hiked up to the climbing tower with Haley and Cindy. Through the intertwining branches, the wind rustled a tune. The sun's rays slipped through the playful shadows. Vibrant green ferns reached out with their creeping tendrils. In the light of day, the stroll was pleasant instead of spooky like it had been during the night game.

It was just the three of them, since Katie was canoeing on the Russian river and Ella was with the guys from their youth group at the paintball course. Melanie really didn't care to know where Bethany was, but she assumed Rachel was with her. What would Bethany do without JB to follow around?

Surprisingly, Cindy was quiet as they walked along. Haley must have noticed, too, since she piped in, "Cat got your tongue?"

Cindy's eyes crossed as she stuck out her tongue to gaze at it. "Nope, my tongue's still attached." She moved her head from side to side. "And I don't see a cat around here."

"Ha, ha. Good one."

"Thank you." Cindy curtsied. "But, Haley, that cliché makes you sound like an old person."

Haley shrugged. "I don't mind. It's a habit I picked up from my grandma like I already told you. I would think you'd be used to it by now."

Melanie side-swiped Cindy. "Hey, don't change the subject. What's bothering you?"

"Oh, Bethany keeps cutting me off and saying how boring I am. It's not like I don't know I'm too talkative, but I can't help myself. When I get excited, I just go and can't stop." She raised her palms up. "What am I supposed to do?"

Haley blew on her lip. "Like you should listen to Bethany. Being talkative is the way God made you. I admit sometimes, you share too much detail," she teased, "but truthfully, that's part of what makes you you!"

"I admit. I'm losing my patience with her." Cindy clenched both fists. "If Bethany doesn't stop, well, . . . I don't know what I'll do."

"You're not the only one." Haley frowned. "She's not even here, and she's ruining things. Let's forget about that stick-in-the-mud."

Cindy groaned. "Stick-in-the-mud? That saying is so ancient, nobody's going to understand you."

"But that's what a cliché is!" Haley countered. "Anyway, you shouldn't open that can of worms if you know what's good for you."

"I'm already too late."

Haley put her hands on her hips. "Oh, cry me a river. Now, you listen here, missy." She pointed at her friend. "You shouldn't bite the hand that feeds you."

Melanie's chest rumbled with laughter. Trying to keep a straight face, she added, "Cindy, you better throw in the towel; you're beating a dead horse."

"Nice!" Haley high-fived her. "A double whammy! Well done!"

"You've converted her," Cindy wailed. "I'm outnumbered!"

Melanie giggled. "Just grin and bear it."

When the trail ended, Haley cocked her head. "Well, Cin, it looks like you're saved just in the nick of time."

In the clearing, a mammoth tower stretched up into the sky, competing with the surrounding treetops. Running patterns of red and gray holds for rock climbing were spaced out along its brown, wooden sides. A few ropes hung down anchored to the top. Besides the safety instructor, they were the first ones there.

The rest of the scheduled group arrived, and the guide advised them on the procedures for climbing. When he was finished, Cindy requested to go first, since she had to meet Vivian to practice for the talent show. Ever the adventurous one, Cindy chose a more difficult route. After donning the equipment and strapping in, Cindy scrambled up quickly like a gecko. A few minutes later, she reached the pinnacle and raised her arm and let out a whoop.

Haley cupped her hands around her mouth. "How did you do that? I can't believe how fast you are."

Overhead, Cindy giggled. "Didn't you know? I'm part monkey." She screeched like one and scratched her armpits. Then she expertly slid down like she was floating from the sky.

Next, it was Melanie's turn. First, she strapped on the yellow helmet and then straddled into the harness. Carefully listening to the instructor, Melanie nodded her understanding as she clipped in. Of the several differing courses, she selected the simplest one. Lifting her head back, she gazed up at the tower looming over her and bit her lip.

Cindy and Haley shouted encouragement. "One rung at a time. You can do it, Melanie."

Drawing a deep breath, she grabbed the hold and launched herself onto the wall. She recalled the guide's words, and instead of pulling with her arms, she pushed herself up with her legs. The first couple of feet were relatively easy, and she created a rhythm. Spotting another hold, she reached out for it and continued her ascent.

Several minutes had passed when she was finally within sight of finishing. Melanie's arms and legs shook. Her body rebelled against the constant strenuous activity. Resting for a moment, a light breeze caressed her face, cooling the sweat dribbling from underneath her helmet. Could she make it? She was so close.

Haley yelled, "Are you done?"

"Nope, I just need a minute."

The instructor reassured her. "Take your time."

It wasn't much farther. She could do it. Blowing out a large breath, she shouted, "Climbing on!"

Slowly, Melanie scaled the last remaining holds. Arriving at the top, Melanie raised her arm and hollered, "Wahoo!" She did it.

Haley laughed at the bottom. "Hurry up! I mean, hurry down. It's my turn."

Heaving a sigh, Melanie complied. Bouncing down the wall dangling from the rope was exhilarating and scary at the same time. She couldn't wait to get her feet back on solid ground.

***

Later, when Melanie and Haley finished archery, the bell rang. They made their way to the fire circle and joined their friends along with the other campers. The Unscripted Hyenas, in their usual outrageous manner, entertained them while making the announcements and distributing the mail. Whenever someone came to collect a letter, one of the guys from the improv group would bow down and hand it to them like the person was royalty. Melanie giggled. Too funny.

Rafé called out, "Bethany Kaslav."

Bethany paraded her way down to the front. Over and over, Rafé called Bethany's name. Putting her hand to her chest with her eyes wide, Bethany did a poor job of acting shocked. Melanie couldn't help herself and rolled her eyes. Who did Bethany think she was impressing? And who were all these people writing to her?

She sighed, upset with herself for being envious of Bethany. But it would be nice to receive some mail. The thought seemed ridiculous, since her family lived so close. Rafé held a large package, and Bethany's name rang out. Melanie's mouth dropped, and she sighed. Next, Katie's name was announced and then some of the other girls, too. Everyone was getting mail except her.

"Miss Melanie Cooper."

What? Her heart raced. Wow! She'd actually gotten a letter.

As she walked down to the front, they called her name again. "Oh, and another one for Miss Melanie Cooper. My, my, it seems someone has a couple admirers."

Melanie blushed when Rafé handed her the letters. She turned, and then Rafé stopped her.

"Wait a minute, young lady. There seems to be one more."

After she retrieved them, Melanie returned to sit with her friends. Three letters. She recognized the handwriting. One was from Megan, and one was from Mom. The last one surprised her—it was from Dad.

13

SOMEONE'S KNOCKING

At the end of Tab Time, Eddie Jay invited those who wanted to make a commitment or rededicate themselves to God to come forward. Several people walked to the front, including Cam. Melanie's heart thumped wildly in her chest. She bit her lip. The pull to join the others in the front was strong, but questions and doubts kept her cemented to the chair.

Before she decided, she wanted to understand it as much as she could. She prayed, *God, I'm not ready yet to make this commitment to You. I don't understand it yet. Give me the chance to learn more about what all this means and what You want to do in my life. Amen.*

The room was silent for a few minutes. Melanie fidgeted in her seat. How long would they have to sit here? Then Eddie Jay closed in prayer.

As the girls gathered their things, Bonnie leaned over. "Melanie, I'd like to talk to you before we go."

"Okay."

Bonnie turned to the others. "Girls, tomorrow are cabin inspections, so we need to clean the rooms tonight. Please start working on them, and Melanie and I will be there to help soon."

When they were alone, Bonnie asked, "Mel, do you have any questions about what Eddie Jay was talking about tonight?"

"Um, not really." She chewed on her lip.

Bonnie tilted her head. "I just wanted to make sure. But if you change your mind, come and talk to me."

"I will. I'm sorry. I hope you're not disappointed," Melanie rushed on.

"Melanie, of course, I want you to make a decision to accept Christ, but that's between you and God. If you commit to Him, it needs to be for the right reason, not to please anyone." Bonnie placed her hand on Melanie's Bible. "May I borrow this?"

Melanie nodded.

As Bonnie riffled through the pages, she said, "Melanie, there is something I feel I need to share with you. Whenever I pray for you, a verse comes to my mind. It's Revelation 3:20." She read, "'Behold, I stand at the door and knock; if anyone hears My voice and opens the door, I will come in to him and will dine with him, and he with Me.'"

"What does that mean?"

Bonnie explained, "I believe the door symbolizes the entrance to our hearts. God wants to have a relationship with us. He calls to us and knocks on the door. Our part is to open it and invite Him in."

From the events earlier this summer, Melanie felt it was true. God had showed her how much He loved and cared for her. But there was something missing that was holding her back. Melanie's heart thumped a steady rhythm, and she sighed.

Pulling out a bookmark from her backpack, Bonnie saved the place in Melanie's Bible. "In case you want to read it again. Also, if you don't mind, I'd like to pray with you."

They bowed their heads.

"Father God, I know You want a personal relationship with Melanie like You do with all of us. Melanie is seeking the truth. Unlock the last pieces of the puzzle, so she may understand the fullness of Who You are and what You have for her. In Jesus' name, amen."

They stood up, and Melanie gave her a hug. "Thank you."

"You're welcome. Now, we better hurry back to help out, especially since most of the mess is yours," she teased.

"Hey!" Melanie opened her mouth to object, but Bonnie was right. Her clothes littered her bunk and the surrounding floor, not to mention all her clutter sprawled across the counter. She had a lot to do before lights out.

When they entered the cabin, it was clean and tidy. On the other side, Cindy, Haley, and Katie sat on the floor near Rachel and Bethany, who were perched on the bed. Ella leaned over from the top bunk. Caught up in a deep conversation and not wanting to interrupt, Melanie and Bonnie stood silently and listened.

"Why do people have to be so nosy? Especially that girl today! My personal life isn't any of her business. I don't see what the big deal is." Haley's voice wobbled. "I was a baby when I was adopted. Mom and Dad are the only parents I've ever known. End of story."

Ella protested. "No, it's not. I've heard your parents share about their struggles having children. God answered their prayers beginning with you and then your little brother. And I'm so glad He did! You're one of my best friends!"

Rachel piped in. "Haley, your adoption story is beautiful. The love you receive from your parents parallels how God sees us, and we should feel like you do—loved and accepted. You're their true child, and so are we to God."

Tears ran down Haley's cheeks, but her face glowed. "Thank you, guys, for saying that! I never feel like people understand, but you do." Her mouth trembled into a smile. "I'll try not to let it bother me anymore when people ask me about being adopted. I can use it as a testimony of God's great love for all of us."

It was beginning to make sense to Melanie. God wanted her to be His child. He loved her like her parents loved her but even more than that, since He had sent His Son, Jesus, to die for her sins.

Bonnie blew her nose. "I'm glad we've been here to witness that special moment. And you did an excellent job on the rooms, too."

Melanie added. "Yeah, thanks for cleaning up all my stuff."

Cindy put her hands on her hips. "You're welcome. But, young lady, you better make your bed in the morning and pick up after yourself."

"Yes, Mom," Melanie said with sarcasm. "But seriously, I really appreciate it." She beamed.

"All right, girls. We need to get ready for bed."

Rachel squeaked out, "We can't yet. Bethany had a great idea."

The girls began talking all at once.

Bonnie laughed. "Maybe one of you can tell me."

Cindy took the lead. "Bethany thought we should give some of the cookies she got from her mom to the judges with a little note. Then, Rachel said we should try to write a poem to go with it."

"Wow, that is a wonderful idea, girls. But we should get ready for bed first." Bonnie raised her finger. "We'll need to be quiet while we work on it, so we don't disturb the cabin next door."

After they changed into their pajamas, Bethany reopened her package and dug out the individually wrapped cookies from the box. "Oh, good. Mom made a baker's dozen. So, each of us can have one, leaving five left over for the judges." She arranged them on the counter.

The large assortment of iced cookies were decorated with a camping theme containing shapes of tents, s'mores, trees, cabins, bears, and a campfire. Each one was colorful and playfully realistic. Melanie chose one of the bears with its cute, brown, fuzzy face. A sweet, buttery flavor with a kick of vanilla filled her mouth when she bit down.

"Mmm, these are delicious." Melanie sighed. "Your mother should sell these. They're so incredibly good!"

Bethany said enthusiastically, "She does. It's called Piper's Pastry Shop. My mom's a classically trained baker, and her pastries are divine. And I'm not just saying that because she's my mom."

Melanie's eyes widened. "I believe you!"

Bethany handed her another cookie. "Here. Have mine. You've got to try one of her chocolate sugar cookies, too."

"Really?" Melanie gasped.

"Yeah, I have them all the time."

"Thanks!"

Bethany continued to talk about the wonderful desserts her mom carried in her shop. This was a different side of Bethany, generous and thoughtful. Finally, it made sense why she was friends with the rest of the girls. Melanie actually liked this Bethany.

Using a page from Bonnie's journal, the girls composed their lighthearted and clever poem. They giggled and laughed, staying up past midnight. When it was finished, each one signed their name. Along with the cookies, Bonnie placed the note on the counter for the judges.

We've made this cabin,
oh so clean,
In hopes of raising
points for Green.
The sugar cookies
are a treat
Showing our spirit
Can't be beat!

Love, Cabins #7 #8

Haley   Melanie

Bethanys

Katie   ELLA

Bonnie

Cindy

Rachel

14

ACCEPTANCE

Seven of them sat at their table during breakfast wearing their matching camp shirts for Spirit Day. Melanie, Katie, Cindy, and Ella were quiet and yawned after their late night. Peppy as usual, Haley made jokes with her dad, Pastor Cliff. But Jane slouched with her coffee, seemingly as tired as the girls.

Haley turned to Jane. "Mom, knock, knock."

Jane huffed. "Who's there?"

"Cher."

"Cher who?"

Haley chuckled out. "Cher would be nice if you weren't so cranky this morning."

"Why, you little tyke." Jane pursed her lips together to keep from smiling.

Pastor Cliff guffawed. "That's my girl." He put his arm around Haley and squeezed.

Jane playfully glared at everyone around the table. "I might not be so grumpy if a certain cabin next door didn't keep waking me up last night with their giggling."

Cindy wearily said, "Sorry about that. We were trying to get extra points for our team for spirit day."

Haley explained to her parents what the girls had done and recited the poem to them. While Haley spoke, Jane pushed a loose strand of hair behind her daughter's ear. Haley rolled her eyes, but the grin she tried to hide revealed she basked in her mother's attention. Gazing at Haley with love and tenderness, it was obvious how they felt about her. She was their daughter, and they were a family. A real family.

Melanie remembered Rachel's comment. Haley was Pastor Cliff and Jane's true child. Her heart thumped. The last piece of the puzzle clicked into place. God wanted to be her Father and have her as a part of His family. Looking around the table at her friends, she realized they already felt like her family. Melanie bit her lip with a smile. She wanted to become a part of God's family, too.

During Soulo Time, Melanie scrambled to the bench outside of the pool area with her Bible. She wanted to read that verse that Bonnie had shared with her after Tab. Remembering what it said, an image formed in her mind of Jesus knocking on the door of her heart. Her heart pounded in response. *Is that You?* A shiver raced along her arms.

With her Bible on her lap, Melanie excitedly tugged on the bookmark trying to find the right page. It slipped out, losing her place. The bookmark fluttered to the ground. When she picked it up, she noticed the words "The Romans Road" in white lettering on the front, along with a picture of a cross.

What was the Romans Road? Turning it over, she read the verses printed on the back. It was the steps to become a Christian. Just what she needed. As she read each one, Melanie nodded in agreement. Yes, she was a sinner. She knew Jesus had died on the cross for her. Melanie also believed God had raised Him from the dead to give her eternal life. But she needed to say it out loud.

She prayed, "Jesus, I know I'm not good, and I'm sorry for all the bad things I have done. Thank You for dying on the cross for me. I believe You are God's Son and that He raised You from the dead. I've been feeling You knocking on the door of my heart. Right now, I'm opening the door and inviting You in." Melanie bit her lip and added, "I want You to be my

Father and I want to be Your child, adopted into Your family. In Jesus' name, amen."

A warm presence washed over her, filling her with light and love. She felt so different and so free! Tears trailed down her cheeks as joyfulness bubbled out of her. Melanie could barely contain her excitement. She needed to tell someone!

After Melanie grabbed her Bible, she marched down to inform Bonnie. Her feet slapped loudly on the path. On the bench across from their cabin, Katie and Bonnie hunched together. Hearing her footsteps, both of them looked up. Katie squealed, jumped up, and ran to Melanie. Bonnie followed closely behind her.

Melanie and Katie threw their arms around each other. Bonnie embraced her, too. The three of them wiped tears from their eyes.

"Katie, Bonnie, I asked Jesus to come into my heart."

"We know!" Katie giggled.

"How?"

"Why do you think we ran up here?" Then she stated proudly, "You didn't notice, but I was watching you at breakfast. Something happened to you there, so I asked Bonnie if we could pray for you during Soulo Time."

Melanie grinned widely. "God answered your prayers."

"He did! But it took you long enough!" Katie elbowed her. "Finally! Now, I can't wait to tell everybody."

"No." Melanie seized her arm. "I don't want anyone else to know yet. I wish there was some way I could tell my mom. Anyway, when I do share with our friends, it should come from me. Katie, you have to promise you won't say anything."

Katie relented. "I promise, but the other girls are your friends, too. They care about you."

"I won't tell either." Bonnie sighed. "Though, I think it will be harder for me to keep it from Brett. He's been praying for you ever since you joined our youth group."

"He has?" Melanie knew Bonnie had been praying for her—and a few other people, too—but Pastor Brett? Why would he care about her?

"Of course, we have. He and I pray for all of the kids in the youth group."

"Now, I feel bad. This would be so much easier if I could talk to my mom."

Bonnie replied, "You can. Come with me." She waved for her to follow. Melanie handed her Bible to Katie.

In the Hospitality Room, Melanie waited while Bonnie spoke to someone in the office. Had it really been only last night she'd talked with Bonnie about making a decision? It seemed so long ago. When Bonnie returned, she nodded to the phone and left. Melanie dialed home.

On the third ring, Mom answered.

"Mom!"

"Melanie, I didn't expect to hear from you. Is everything okay?" Concern edged her voice.

"Yes," Melanie squeaked. "I have something important to tell you." She cleared her throat. "I asked Jesus into my heart today."

"Oh, honey," she gasped. "I'm so happy. I've been praying for this day. If my ankle wasn't broken, I'd be jumping up and down. So, what happened? What prompted you to make this decision?"

The bell rang, signaling cabin discussion time.

Melanie groaned. "Oh no. Mom, I have to go, but I promise I'll tell you *everything* when I get home."

"Then, I can't wait! Have fun with your friends. Bye, sweetheart. I love you!"

"Love you, too!"

"And, Melanie, I'm proud of you."

Melanie smiled gleefully. "Thanks, Mom."

Instead of walking back, Melanie wanted to sing and dance, celebrating what God had done for her. Love, joy, and peace welled up within her. How could she feel so many things at one time? With this much happiness, nothing could dampen her mood—not even Bethany. Her heart pounded wildly. Melanie giggled. Inside, it felt like God was pleased, too.

15

ANSWERED PRAYERS

Coming up the hill, Melanie was the last one from her cabin to arrive. Now that she'd told her mom, she didn't mind revealing her exciting news to her friends, except for Bethany. It was going to be hard sharing something so personal with her around, but maybe she'd give Bethany another chance. After all, it might not be so bad, since Bethany had been nice to her last night with the cookies.

As Melanie sank down on the bench, she tried to hide her smile. She glanced at Bonnie and Katie, who beamed. Neither of them could contain their glee. No matter how hard they tried, they wouldn't be able to keep the secret for long. Melanie chuckled.

Surprisingly observant, Cindy caught on to their expressions. "What's going on? Did something happen?" Her voice rose.

"Yeah, you're right, Cin." Haley placed her hand on her hip. "One of you better spill the beans."

Both Bonnie and Katie turned their heads toward Melanie.

Cindy squealed and embraced Melanie. Haley and Rachel gasped loudly. Ella jumped up yelling a yippee. Then they hugged Melanie, too.

When they pulled away, Melanie raised her arms out. "Am I wearing a sign?"

Bethany grumbled, "I don't understand. What am I missing?"

"I guess it's not so obvious to all of us," Cindy replied.

Melanie lifted her head. "During Soulo Time, I asked Jesus into my heart."

"Oh." Bethany gave Melanie a half-hearted pat. "That's nice. I did that last year, so I can go to Heaven."

Melanie didn't know what to say. That wasn't the reason she'd accepted Jesus as her Savior. Heaven was a bonus. It was what He'd done for her on the cross and the love He gave her, the joy she had in knowing God was her Father and being adopted as His child into His family. Her relationship with Him was the most important part. A tremble rolled down her back.

During the discussion time, Melanie explained the steps which had led her to make her decision and her struggles with understanding God cared about her and loved her. As she concluded, Melanie locked eyes with Haley. She shared the impact of Haley's adoption and how it mirrored the type of relationship God desired to have with her.

When she was finished, most of them were in tears. Haley hugged her again tightly. Melanie squeezed back and released her. Bonnie passed out tissues. The girls wiped their eyes and blew their noses.

Melanie laughed awkwardly. "Why are you guys crying? Isn't this supposed to make you happy?"

"Because it's beautiful," Rachel said breathlessly.

"And an answer to our prayers," Katie added.

Melanie smiled so wide, her cheeks hurt. "The joy inside me is overflowing. I feel different, filled with love and light."

Cindy's eyes brightened. "This is the best thing that has happened this week."

"Yes, most definitely." Ella's shoulders rocked.

Haley put her arm around Melanie. "This is such great news. Wait until the entire youth group hears about it."

Melanie's eyes widened. "Please, don't tell. I mean, it's all new to me and very special. I want to be the one who shares it. You guys understand, right?"

The girls nodded.

Bonnie handed Melanie a purple pen. "You need to write down this date in your Bible. It's your spiritual birthday." She held up her own Bible. "I already put it in mine. It also reminds me God answered our prayers."

Melanie's name was written there with today's date. It warmed Melanie's heart. She was so lucky—no, not lucky, blessed. She was blessed to have such wonderful, caring friends. But they were more than that now; they were family.

***

After rec, Pastor Brett came over to their lunch table and stood next to Bonnie. "Is this seat taken, gorgeous?"

"I'm saving it for my husband," Bonnie replied.

"Lucky him." Pastor Brett wiggled his eyebrows.

Melanie and Katie giggled.

"Yep, he is." Bonnie winked.

He laughed, bent down, kissed his wife on the cheek, and then squeezed his large frame onto the bench next to her.

Cindy and Trevor elbowed each other playfully as they placed their trays noisily on the table. Taking the last available spots, JB and Cam settled across from Melanie and Katie. Melanie's heart skipped a beat. Hunkering down, she munched on her taco and avoided eye contact with JB. Would she ever conquer being nervous around him?

Talking between bites, Pastor Brett asked, "What adventures will you girls be up to this afternoon? After lunch, the boys and I will be heading out to ride the scooters."

Bonnie voiced concern. "They're so dangerous. I hope none of you get hurt flying down the hill on one of those things."

"But that's the thrill of it," Trevor defended with a half shrug.

Cindy shook her head at her brother's remark. "To answer your question, Pastor Brett, I have to practice for the talent show tonight. But later"—she glanced at Melanie—"if someone wanted to, I planned to swim."

Cam interjected, "A dip in the pool would be sweet if we have enough time. But you see, I gotta practice my skills for the foosball tournament tomorrow if JB and I want to win." Enthusiastically, he added, "You guys should come and watch us."

JB nodded and furtively glanced at Melanie. "Yeah, you should. Our only real competition is from Adam and his partner. It will be hard to beat Ella, since she's the best foosball player in the youth group."

"Wait. What?" Melanie pulled her head back. "Ella and Adam are on the same team?"

"Yeah, they always play together."

Ew, why would Ella do that? Of all the people she could choose from, why would Ella want to be a teammate with Adam? Spending time with him would be the worst. It didn't make any sense. There had to be a reason.

JB announced proudly, "Cam made up our team name." He turned to Cam. "Let's see if they get it."

"We're the Lords of the Silver Rings." They said it together as they raised their left hands, displaying the silver ring each had on their fourth finger.

Katie's eyes grew big. "How Tolkien of you."

Cam clapped his hands. "She got it!"

"I should. He's one of my favorite fantasy authors besides Lewis and Lawhead." She scooted forward in her seat.

"No way! Are you serious?" Cam spoke excitedly. "I've read most of their books. What are your favorites?"

While the others carried on their own conversations, Melanie and JB chatted about swimming. Even though, she didn't intend to, Melanie gushed on and on. Here was someone who loved her sport as much as she did. He didn't seem to mind, but he kept tilting his head and squinting at her. Her nervousness returned, but she was slightly annoyed, too.

Finally, she questioned him. "Why do you keep looking at me funny? Do I have something on my face? Or am I talking too much?"

"No! Uh, sorry." He sucked in a breath. "It's just . . . there's something different about you."

Melanie bit her lip and smiled. "Possibly."

16

FAVORITE SPOT

After lunch, Melanie followed Katie along one of the paved paths. Turning onto a dirt trail lined with older cabins, they carefully maneuvered down an embankment into a partial clearing. Orange pine needles, fallen branches, and exposed tree roots littered the ground. The dense canopy of lime and bottle green leaves reflected in the waters of the creek as it snaked across the landscape hugged by the gray, rocky beach.

A lone, red cottage connected by a footbridge peeked out from the overgrown thicket on the opposite bank. The richness of the wooded surroundings perfumed the damp air, while a swarm of tiny bugs danced in the sunlight. As the creek trickled along, Melanie and Katie sat silently on an aged, toppled tree, enjoying the tranquility. Somewhat secluded, Katie's favorite spot felt sacred and enchanting.

Melanie sighed. She understood why Katie loved this place, and she'd grown to love it, too—not this exact spot, but the one a couple miles away in her own backyard. The water had flowed from behind her house only a short while ago. At home, she would always be able to experience this peaceful atmosphere.

Tilting her head, Melanie said, "I can understand why you like to be alone here."

"But I don't feel alone. That's the point." Katie breathed deeply. "This is where I feel the closest to God. I can be still and sense Him."

"I feel Him, too." Melanie paused and then continued softly, "Remember when we sang the finger candle song?"

"Ohhh, you mean, 'This Little Light of Mine'?"

"That's the one." Melanie bit her lip. "While we sang, you touched my finger. It seemed like you were passing on the light and love of Jesus to me."

Katie's eyes teared. "Really?"

Melanie nodded. "You've been showing me God's love throughout our friendship. It radiates out from you."

"I don't feel like I did anything, since you only started going to church after you moved."

"Don't be silly. I know you've been praying for me, and it finally worked." Melanie beamed. "Thanks for not giving up on me."

"Of course, you're my best friend. And now, we're even more—we're sisters in Christ. You're officially part of God's family. I've been waiting so long for this. I know God and the angels are rejoicing in Heaven."

"They are?"

"Yes, it says so in the Bible. And I want to celebrate, too. Hmm, what should we do?" Katie paused. "Maybe we should go to the camp store and get something to wear that matches?"

"We already have our camp shirts."

Katie furrowed her brow and then stammered, "I-I've got it. How about some kind of jewelry? Maybe we can even find something with a cross on it."

"Oh yes, that would be so cool!"

"Then we can wear it when we're apart."

Melanie sighed. "I don't really want to think about that."

"I don't either, but it's been on my mind." Katie pursed her lips. "Truthfully, I'm dreading going back to school."

"You are? But you know everybody."

Katie exhaled heavily. "That's just it. Everyone has friends already. Where will I fit in? It's always been just you and me."

"I'm sorry. I've been so selfish." Melanie lowered her head. "When we moved, I thought only about what I would miss. I didn't realize you'd be losing something, too."

"Mel, it's okay. With God's help, I'll adjust. Maybe you could pray for me?"

Melanie's eyes widened. "I'd love to do that!"

Katie laid her hand on Melanie's arm. "I'm not too upset about it, since I realize this was God's plan all along. Having you come to know Christ has made everything worth it."

"You really mean that, don't you?"

"I do!" Katie stood, brushing herself off and hauled Melanie up. "Now, we've got things to do, and we should hurry, so afterward, we can spend some time in your favorite spot—the pool."

***

After swimming, Melanie and her friends chomped down on nachos as they sat at one of the patio tables on the deck in the main area. Bethany hogged the conversation, rambling on and on about how she'd spent the summer. She described in detail the fashion shows she'd attended and the new clothes her dad had bought her. Bored, Melanie played with her new bracelet, which matched Katie's.

Approaching them, Fiona, one of the girl's from youth group, announced, "Did you guys hear what happened?" Her tone held a note of gossip.

"We don't know until you tell us what it is," Haley said with her usual sarcastic charm.

"Someone from our church got really hurt riding the scooters. They're taking them to the hospital."

Haley's eye widened. "Oh no!"

Cindy's voice quivered. "Trevor was . . . "

Ella interrupted. "Did they say who it was?"

"One of the campers. That's all I heard." Fiona shrugged and walked away.

Patting Cindy's shoulder, Ella said, "It can't be your brother, since he's one of the counselors."

Katie proposed, "We should pray for them right now."

The girls agreed.

She prayed, "Dear Lord, please be with the person who got hurt. Don't let their injury be serious. Heal them quickly. In Jesus' name . . . "

"Amen," they all said.

Cindy rose. "Sorry, guys, I've got to do something. I won't feel better until I *know* it wasn't Trevor who was hurt."

"I'll go with you," Haley volunteered. "Maybe if we find my parents, they might know something."

Melanie stated, "We'll all go with you."

17

TALENT SHOW

Together, they found Bonnie returning from the parking lot. The girls rushed up to her with Bethany trailing slowly behind.

With her hand on her chest, Cindy asked Bonnie, "Do you know who got hurt on the scooters?"

She nodded. "It was Adam."

As she exhaled, relief flooded Cindy's features.

Phew. It wasn't JB, Trevor, or Cam. Melanie hadn't realized she'd been holding her breath, too. Maybe she should be more concerned, but it was difficult to sympathize, since it was Adam.

"What?" Ella's voice trembled as it grew higher. "Is he going to be okay?"

Bonnie put a comforting arm around Ella's shoulders. "Yes, Ella. Brett's with him. He scraped up his knee and will probably need stitches. He's fine, otherwise."

Why was Ella so upset, crying over Adam? Melanie mumbled, "What's wrong with Ella?"

Katie whispered back, "She likes Adam."

"Ohh! Gross! No way!" Melanie grimaced. "How do you know?"

"Isn't it obvious?"

It hadn't been until now. Ella spent a lot of time with the guys. Melanie had assumed it was her love of sports. But it made sense. As the best foosball player, she'd chosen Adam as her partner. What did she see in him? He was so mean. But maybe there was something more to Adam. After all, he was friends with JB.

***

With some of her friends in tow, Melanie clumped up the stairs of the tabernacle for the talent show. The building was another cabin-like structure with wood walls and giant rafters but with rows of windows allowing views of the beautiful nature surrounding them. Centered above the stage was a round, stained glass window. On the opposite side of the platform sat a grand piano. At the instrument, Vivian, Melanie's neighbor, warmed up on the keys.

When Vivian saw her, she quit mid-song and joined the girls. Embracing Melanie, she said, "Oh,

Mel, your mom told me you made a decision to follow Jesus. That's wonderful! I'm so happy."

Melanie grinned. "Me, too!"

With her arm around Melanie's shoulder, Vivian turned to Cindy. "How's my star pupil?"

Cindy bit her lip. "Nervous."

"Let's run a few scales before it starts," Vivian suggested.

As the minutes ticked by, campers and counselors began to fill the seats. Claiming the first row of the center section, the girls saved places for the rest of their cabin. The noisy clatter of excitement rose as more and more people arrived, including Bonnie, Rachel, and Bethany. Cindy finished practicing and took the remaining seat next to Melanie.

Reaching out, Melanie squeezed Cindy's sweaty hand. "You're going to be great."

Rafé took the microphone and went onstage. As the emcee of the show, Rafé cracked a few jokes. Then he announced, "Campers, we have some great entertainment for you this evening. Our first performer is Cindy . . . wow, this is a long last name." Glancing at the crowd, he said, "I think I'll make this easy on myself. Cindy D. will be singing for us." He clapped.

A few sporadic claps echoed from the audience as Cindy gingerly exited the row. At the same time, Vivian headed up to the piano. Taking the microphone from Rafé, Cindy stood in the middle of the platform. Her voice wobbled as she introduced Vivian as her accompanist and then nodded to her.

As Vivian played the intro, a confident smile graced Cindy's face. Her strong, angelic voice rang out sweetly throughout the auditorium. Melanie and those around her were swept up into the music. It was breathtakingly beautiful. Cindy's talent shone, and she even looked the part of a professional singer with her stylish pixie cut and chic outfit.

Cindy continued to belt out the high notes masterfully as the song reached its crescendo. An awed silence rested on the crowd when the song ended; then they jumped up with a roar of applause. Standing on a chair, Trevor pumped his arms and hollered. Cindy's face glowed as she bowed. She motioned toward Vivian, who inclined her head in acknowledgment. Melanie enthusiastically cheered for her friend.

After Cindy's show-stopping performance, the acts continued with a couple of musicians, a comedian, and a surprisingly good magician duo. Other favorites were a youth group, who entertained them with a skit rivaling

The Unscripted Hyenas in hilarity, and a guy who tooted a song on his kazoo. At the end, prizes were awarded. With no surprise to anyone, Cindy received first place. The crowd once again thundered their approval and delight.

***

In the dining hall after the talent show, Melanie munched on popcorn. All of the girls were with her except for Katie, who was on the phone downstairs talking with her family. Since their table was close to the double doors, multiple people stopped by to congratulate Cindy. She beamed and blushed over their attention.

Rachel said, "Cin, you really need to start singing at church—maybe in the choir, or on the worship team, or a solo." She popped a kernel in her mouth.

Cindy pursed her lips. "I might. I need to talk to Vivian and see what she says. But I'm not sure, since I haven't decided yet what kind of music I want to pursue."

Haley placed her cup down. "You should try out for one of those TV talent shows. Then after you win and become famous, I'll tell everyone we're friends."

Sticking her tongue out, Cindy teased, "I'm offended. Why can't you brag to everyone I'm your friend now?"

Haley threw a piece of popcorn at her and grinned. "The key word is *famous*."

Cindy frowned. "I see how it is."

Two campers interrupted them, but these ones wanted Cindy's autograph. Awkwardly, she obliged. They left, excited and giggling.

"Ah, that was weird," Cindy confessed. "I don't know if I could get used to that."

"It seems like the famous part is starting already." Haley pointed to Cindy and spoke loudly. "Hey, look, everybody. She's my friend."

The girls laughed, all except for Bethany, who just rolled her eyes.

"I met tons of *real* celebrities on my trip," Bethany bragged. "Most of them are my dad's clients."

With a snarky expression, Haley remarked, "Fascinating."

"Yes, it is," Bethany retorted back, missing the barb. "Camp is so boring compared to the wonderful parties I attended."

"It's a wonder you came." Haley shook her head.

"Duh! For JB."

"Camp is not boring!" Ella defended, then added, "There's tons of activities, and some you could do with JB. Paintball was a blast!"

"It hasn't helped Adam notice you."

A collective gasp burst out from the girls.

Ella's face flamed. She stood, scrambling to grab her snack. Tears sprang to her eyes as she darted away.

Scowling at Bethany, Haley called after her, "Wait up, El, I'm coming with you."

"Do you have to be so insensitive?" Anger dripped from Cindy's voice. "You don't need to say everything you think."

Bethany snapped back, "Like you should talk? Oh, wait, that's what you do—babbling incessantly all the time."

Cindy's face reddened. "What's happened to you? I've heard your snide remarks during our cabin discussions. Sure, I may be a little over-talkative sometimes, but that's the way God made me. At least, I care about my friends."

Bethany looked down her nose. "I care, but I'm not taking advice about boys from someone like Ella."

"What do you mean?" Cindy asked.

"You know what I mean." Bethany rolled her eyes. "She's big."

Melanie's mouth fell open. Rachel frowned and shook her head.

Cindy clenched her fists. "Do you even hear yourself? And Ella's *not* big. She's tall and muscular."

"Call it what you want." Bethany shrugged.

Cindy rose. "This is ridiculous. I've tolerated your hurtful comments to me, but this is over the top, even for you. You don't make fun of your friends; you build them up. I'm not sure if we should be friends anymore."

Bethany turned to Rachel for support. "Can you believe this?"

"Yes, I warned you," Rachel huffed, shaking her head. "I can't believe what you said about Ella. She's always been kind to you. Bethany, the mean things you say have consequences. I don't know if I can put up with it anymore either."

As the three girls began to walk away, Cindy turned back. "By the way, you really should return Melanie's *missing* swimsuit before someone accuses you of stealing it."

Bethany flushed and stammered, "I-i-it just got lost for a bit."

They exited.

Sitting on the benches downstairs, Cindy elbowed Rachel. "Wow, Rach, I didn't know you had it in you."

"I'm not proud of myself, and I'm not happy with you either, Cin."

"What? Bethany got exactly what she deserved."

"Maybe, but you don't get it. She's not strong like the rest of us. And you don't know what happens with her dad. That's why she acts up." She sighed. "But this year is different. It's been worse since Melanie arrived."

Flabbergasted, Melanie flicked her head. "What? What did I do?"

"Nothing, but look at it from her point of view." Rachel threw her hand back. "She went away for the summer and came back to friends who seem to prefer you over her. She feels like you've taken her place." She sighed again. "And don't get me started about JB. We can all tell he likes you."

Melanie blushed.

Rachel covered her face with her hand, then pushed herself up. "Oh, there's so many things you don't know. I need to cool off and pray about it." She left.

Melanie and Cindy remained quiet, taking in everything. Neither of them, nor anyone else in their circle, really understood Bethany's life, except for Rachel. Her revelations were practically unbelievable but were starting to make sense.

Katie ran up to them. "Hey, what's going on? Where is everybody? Did I miss anything?"

With eyes wide, Melanie said, "You could say that."

18

NEW LIFE

Bonnie shook Melanie awake for morning worship. Even though she was tired from all the activities, Melanie bounced out of bed, eager to learn all she could about Jesus. After changing quickly and pulling her hair into a ponytail, Melanie donned her sweatshirt and was ready to go. Exiting the door quietly so she wouldn't wake the other girls, Melanie stepped out into the crisp, morning air with Bonnie following. Full of enthusiasm, Melanie bounded down the stairs to the main area and over to the Fireside Room with Bonnie hurrying to catch up with her.

Inside, two rows of folding chairs were lined up in a semi-circle. In front, Trevor perched on a stool with his guitar. Several people filled the seats. Pastor Brett and another guy in a baseball cap lounged in the back. Melanie gasped when she recognized JB. She didn't know he would be here.

Bonnie came up beside her and then guided Melanie over toward the guys. Bonnie plopped down next to her husband. On the other side of Pastor Brett, JB caught her eye and grinned. Melanie sent him a small wave as she took the chair next to Bonnie.

One of the counselors, Pastor Matt from the blue team, opened in prayer. Then Trevor strummed his guitar, leading them in a song. Everyone stood. Melanie sensed a shared connectedness with those around her. A kind of camaraderie she'd never experienced before even when she'd been on her swim team.

Focusing her attention on the worship, Melanie sang along to the lyrics, which were displayed on the back wall. As the familiar tune continued to play, the words brought an understanding to her of the love God had for her. Closing her eyes, her heart soared with the music. An inner shiver coursed through her body. Was this what it felt like to have God living inside her? If it was, it was truly amazing. A warm peace settled over her. She sighed with contentment.

After several songs, their time was over. Why did it have to end? She could sing praises all day long. Melanie smiled to herself. She really meant it. This feeling—this closeness to God—she didn't want it to fade.

But how could she remain near to Him every day? Remembering the first sermon she'd heard at youth group, Pastor Brett spoke of a relationship with God. That's what she needed to have. But how could she do that? Maybe she should ask Bonnie.

As Bonnie and Melanie strolled back to the cabin after morning worship, Bonnie said, "Mel, I wanted to talk to you about your decision yesterday."

"Sure, go ahead."

"When you become a new believer, it's important to understand your faith. We call it discipleship. I wondered—actually, I hoped—I could disciple you. That is, if you wanted."

Melanie smiled and bit her lip. "Is that how you develop a closer relationship with God?"

"Yes, it is. But before you give me an answer, you should pray about it."

Melanie beamed. "But I already know. I'd love for you to teach me more about Jesus."

A delighted grin spread across Bonnie's face. "I'll need to speak to your parents for their permission, and if they agree, we need to figure out a time to meet on a regular basis."

When they returned to their room, all of the girls were ready for breakfast. As Melanie quickly went to make her bed, a familiar blue color peeked out from the covers. It was her missing bathing suit. Bethany had returned it. She was so glad to have it back. Melanie packed it into her suitcase without saying a word.

***

Instead of Soulo Time and cabin discussions, seminars were on the schedule. Ever since she'd heard about Bonnie and Jane's seminar on missions, Melanie had wanted to attend. Of her friends, it seemed only Haley would be going. When they were dismissed from Tab Time, Melanie went downstairs, through the double doors, and into the Kinser Room.

Around the perimeter, circular and rectangular tables were set up. Jenna, one of the girls from youth group who was in Jane's cabin, sat at a table covered with a bunch of envelopes. Another girl's table had mounds of white sheets. At the back, Haley peeked out from behind a table with two stacks of vibrant fabrics on it. Melanie headed toward Haley until she pointed Melanie over to the rows of chairs in the center. Surprisingly, Rachel was here, too, so Melanie joined her instead.

Bonnie and Jane stood at the front. Even though people continued to stream in, Bonnie began the presentation. "Welcome to our seminar on missions. As many of you know, one of our church's core values is sending out missionaries, who share the Good News of Jesus to other countries. Our weekly women's group prays for them, but we also like to help by supporting their ministries, whether financially or with their outreach projects."

Jane spoke next. "Today, you will be partnering with us on three of those projects. First off"—she motioned to the side—"Jenna is in charge of our stamp collection, one of our easier activities. And Peyton is running our bandage station for our hospital in Africa. It's a lot of ripping and rolling. Quite fun! My daughter, Haley, is in charge of the pattern-cutting station to make dresses for little girls."

Haley stood and then unfurled an adorable outfit. It was mint green with orange and pink flowers. The solid, bright orange pocket had a cute, white button sewn on it. There were many *oohs* and *ahs*. Melanie would've loved to have had a dress like that when she was little.

"Our last station is sewing. Bonnie and I will be manning it. As you can guess, our job is to sew the dresses. We have two extra machines if anyone knows how to sew. Or Bonnie or I can teach you, if you want to learn."

"Oh, a few more things I forgot to mention," Bonnie added. "If you'd like to do these projects at home, the instructions are provided at each station. And also"—she touched a brightly colored tote bag on the front table—"these beautiful and unique craft items are for sale. All proceeds will go toward these ministries. Next to them, we have missionary cards, so you can pray for a specific family and the country they serve. Also, we'll be open during free time, in case you want to keep helping. Okay, I think that's all. Let's have some fun!"

Melanie asked, "Rachel, which one should we do first?"

Rachel's mouth shifted, and she quietly said, "Actually, I'm going to help on the sewing machines."

"I didn't know you knew how to sew. Wow, I'm impressed."

Rachel blushed.

On her own, Melanie trimmed stamps at Jenna's station. Afterward, she moved over to Peyton's and made bandages. Melanie cut and ripped sheets and then rolled and tied the strips. Next, she wanted to do the patterns with Haley, but her table was too crowded. Opting to spend time with Rachel, Melanie scooted into a seat next to her.

Rachel glanced over with a shy smile. "Let me finish this hem, and then I can teach you the basics."

Melanie replied, "What's a hem?"

Rachel giggled. "You really are a novice. A hem is the edge of the clothing and where you determine the length of a garment."

"If you don't mind, I'd rather watch and have you explain what you're doing."

"Okay," Rachel agreed. Then she sighed. "I'm glad we have this time together." She paused, nervous. "You see, I need to apologize. I knew Bethany took your bathing suit, but I didn't say anything. I'm really sorry."

Melanie shrugged. "At least she returned it."

"Actually, that was me. I wanted to make sure you got it back." Rachel pulled off the material from the sewing machine and snipped the dangling threads.

"Thanks." Melanie bit her lip. "Rachel, you shouldn't feel bad about it. I mean it's hard to stand up against your best friend."

Tears huddled in Rachel's eyes. "Thank you for understanding."

"Are you and Bethany friends again?"

Rachel took a deep breath. "Kind of." She was silent for a few seconds. "I won't completely abandon her. Let's just say it's complicated, and I need to keep praying about it."

Melanie put a hand on Rachel's shoulder. "I'll pray, too."

19

DYE WARS

Dressed in scruffy, light-colored clothes, Melanie headed up with the rest of the campers for their last day of rec—dye wars. Already warm from traipsing up the hill, Melanie emerged onto the ballfield, which was as hot as a furnace. Sweat broke out on her skin. She blew out from her bottom lip to try to cool her face.

The girls found a spot beneath the trees and fanned themselves in the shade. Across the lawn on the four corners were gigantic, black garbage cans. Each had a sign stating the name of a team. Near the bottom of the cans were clear plastic bags filled with large, bright red cups.

A horn-like sound blared from Nelson's megaphone. Gaining their attention, he instructed them to move into the designated areas. When they were settled, he announced they would have a cheering competition. Taking up the challenge, a spirit contest broke out, which moved back and forth between the groups as each one tried to outdo the others. Pastor Cliff saddled Haley on his shoulders. Melanie yelled along with the rest of the gang on the green team. The shouts roared in her ears.

Nelson's voice crackled loudly. "Great job, everyone. Now, it's time for dye wars." Interrupted by their excitement, he then resumed. "The object for dye wars is simple. Using the cups provided, scoop out your team's dyed water and splash as many of the other teams' members as you can. We will be judging which color is most predominately featured on each person. Any questions? I didn't think so. All right, let's go!" His megaphone's siren blared again.

Melanie's team swarmed the garbage cans, filling their cups. When she finally got a turn, Melanie bent over and bailed out some of the green water. Then she entered the fray. Immediately, blue water spurted into her face. She wiped it off and then tossed the contents of her cup onto the offending boy's chest. Green streaked across his t-shirt. She laughed.

Melanie darted around the field, infiltrating the opposing teams' territory needing to retreat often for refills. Her team changed tactics. When she returned to their side, someone took her empty cup and handed her a fresh one. Weapon ready, Melanie continued her onslaught. Soaked, Melanie's clothes stuck to her skin but also made the stifling temperature bearable.

Her legs burned from exertion. Out of breath, Melanie's heart raced. Every movement was tiring, but she was having so much fun. Grabbing another cup from Bonnie, Melanie reentered the fight. Before Nelson sounded the signal to end the game, Melanie had gotten in a few more strategic shots.

Practically panting, Melanie stood with her team as they lined up in rows to be inspected. Melanie bit her lip to hold back a giggle when she saw JB's blond hair streaked in multiple colors. Melanie squeezed out the water from her ponytail. Everyone who'd participated—campers and counselors alike—were drenched from head to toe. No one had escaped unscathed—even Bethany, who'd tried to hide.

When the rec leaders finished scoring, they were dismissed. Buckets of chilled bottled water had been provided for them. The campers ransacked the pails and then returned to the main campgrounds. Of her cabinmates, Ella was the only one who remained up at the ballfield with her.

Exhausted from their activities, Melanie stretched out on one of the benches and covered her face with her arm. After resting, she'd snatch a water and then make the long trek down the hill. But something cool and wet tapped against her skin. Melanie lifted her arm and opened her eyes. Shading her from the sun, Ella smiled and handed her a bottle.

"Thanks." Melanie grasped it and sat up.

"You did great today, Mermaid!" Ella gave her a high-five. "You were unstoppable."

Melanie snickered. "I'm paying for it now. I don't know if I can move my legs. But it was worth it!"

Adam, who was settled in a chair near them, said, "Yeah, you weren't too bad, Fishface."

Melanie ignored him. Before, she'd been feeling somewhat sorry for Adam, since he couldn't join in with rec. He'd had to watch from the sidelines because of his knee injury. Dye wars was one of the highlights of camp. But he wouldn't get much sympathy from her if he was going to call her names.

Adam groaned. "I'm so thirsty. Can someone get me a water?"

Ella pursed her lips. "I will if you say please."

Over-dramatically, he moaned, "Please."

Ella retrieved two bottles. One she gave to Adam, which he greedily took from her without any gratitude. She unscrewed the other and then stopped. She waited while he noisily gulped down his drink.

Adam complained, "I wish I could have played. I missed out on all the fun."

Ella smiled mischievously and raised the bottle. "Let's remedy that." She poured the ice cold water over his head.

He jolted, and his eyes widened. "Hey!"

Ella chuckled and shrugged. "You're the one who wanted to participate." She tilted her head. "I won't move if you want to get me back."

"Tempting, but I better not." He patted down his wet hair.

"Smart," she teased.

Pastor Brett zoomed up in the golf cart and offered them a ride. Adam ambled into the passenger seat. The girls hopped into the back. At the bottom of the hill, Ella and Melanie climbed out and thanked him.

Shaking her head, Melanie said, "Ella, why didn't Adam get mad at you?"

With a smug expression, she replied, "He wouldn't dare. He's too competitive and wants to win the foosball tournament. I don't have to choose him to play with me."

"But wouldn't you pick him anyway, since you know . . ." Melanie was too embarrassed to say more.

Ella blushed. "Yeah, I would, but he doesn't know that." She raised her eyebrows and gave Melanie an impish grin.

They laughed.

20

CUT IT OUT

During free time, Melanie ambled along the trail to the gym complex. Even though it was her last opportunity to swim, she was too worn out and finally dry after dye wars. Anyway, she'd rather help with the mission projects. Now, she'd have a chance to visit Haley's station.

In the main hallway, loud noises assaulted her from the rec room. Melanie bit her lip. She'd completely forgotten about the foosball tournament. Maybe she should pop her head in for a few minutes, since JB and Cam had invited her to watch.

The crowd was centered around the foosball table intensely focused on the game in progress. The ball rattled, and the bars rumbled as the competitors played. Melanie drew closer to the action. Bethany leaned close to JB. When she saw Melanie, she glared and crossed her arms. Melanie sighed heavily. She had better things to do so she made her escape.

In the Kinser Room, several people worked at the different stations. Some were cutting stamps, and others were ripping and rolling sheets into bandages. Jane, Bonnie, and Rachel manned the sewing machines, busily working on the stack of dress patterns piled high on the table. Another girl helped, too, but she had her head down. The girl glanced up from her project and smiled. It was Haley.

Melanie blurted out, "You can sew?" Her eyes widened.

"Hey, don't look so surprised." Haley pursed her lips.

"Shock is more like it. How come you guys all know how to sew?"

Rachel answered, "Our moms are in the women's group. We wanted to help on the projects, too, so they taught us."

Melanie confessed, "Earlier, I was nervous about learning how to sew. But if Haley can do it, so can I."

They laughed.

Jane added, "It's about time our Haley met her match in sarcasm and teasing."

Haley tilted her head. "But the Bible says that, 'Iron sharpens iron,' so you might want to rethink that statement, Mom."

Jane sighed deeply. "Oh, my girl."

Melanie put her hands on her hips. "Haley, I want to learn how to cut out the dress patterns. Will you teach me?"

"Maybe, if you're nice to me. Okay," she replied without hesitation. Then she walked over to her station and pointed to the mound of colorful fabrics. "First, you'll need to pick out your material."

There were so many options, but the floral prints were the prettiest. It was so hard to choose between them, but Melanie finally settled on one with daisies and a blue background. Haley decided on a pink one with little red roses. The two girls stood side by side.

Haley handed Melanie a packet with a pattern and directions. "If you follow the diagram, it will show you where to position all the pieces. Each one is labeled. But for now, you can just copy me." Haley folded the cloth in half lengthwise. Melanie imitated her. Taking the thin, beige tissue paper of the pattern, Haley laid them out on the material, almost like a puzzle. She smoothed them out gently to remove any wrinkles.

Haley placed a small container of pins between them. With one of the pins, Haley secured the pieces together. "You want to make sure you fasten it all the way through." She lifted up to show Melanie the underside. When they'd completed that step, they moved on to cutting. The scissors felt large and heavy in her hands. Melanie snipped carefully along the edges while Haley sliced through hers. Done quickly, Haley cleaned up her scraps and checked on Melanie's progress.

Melanie straightened her shoulders for a short break. "You make this seem so simple."

"It is. Of course, my mom and I've made so many of these, I could probably do them in my sleep."

Maybe this was something she and her mom could do together. They'd probably have to wait, though, until Mom's broken ankle healed. But what about Megan? Perhaps, her sister would be interested in it, too, since she was into clothes and fashion.

Melanie finished the last piece. "That was a lot more work than I thought it would be." She stretched her cramped hand and shook it out.

"You'll get faster at it, but yeah, that one took you, like, forever." Haley winked.

Melanie wailed, "You're so bad!"

"You know I'm only kidding. Truthfully, I wish everyone I taught was as detailed and meticulous as you."

"Ah, you can be very sweet when you want to be." Melanie raised an eyebrow and grinned.

"Oh, a backhanded compliment. Nice one. Seriously, though, if I ever go too far in my teasing, let me know. You're my friend, and I *never* want to hurt you."

"The same goes for me." Melanie picked up the pieces of the dress carefully and carried them over to the sewing table. "I want to do another one, but I'll be right back. Nature calls."

Later, just as Melanie was about to push the door to exit the restroom, she heard a loud, familiar, male voice in the hallway, which made her hesitate. Footsteps drew closer. It sounded as though two people were arguing. She didn't want to get into the middle of it. Feeling trapped, Melanie backed up against the wall and waited.

"I mean it, Bethany. You've got to stop following me everywhere."

Oh, no. It was JB and Bethany. This was the last place she wanted to be. But where could she go? There was no place to hide.

Bethany flirted, "I'd stop if you agreed to go on a date with me."

Wow, Bethany was bold. Where did she get such confidence? Melanie would never announce her feelings about someone, especially to that person face to face.

"I've already told you I've made a commitment to God and also to my parents. I won't date until I'm ready to get married," JB said with determination.

"Don't you think that's a bit extreme? I mean, what's the big deal?" She huffed. "Anyway, I find that hard to believe, since I know there's one girl you'd make an exception for."

"It doesn't matter if I like someone or not; I'm not changing my mind about my vow."

"We'll see." Bethany's tone held doubt.

A door slammed, and then it was quiet. Melanie listened for a minute or two. Figuring the coast was clear, she opened the door and scrambled across the empty hallway. Melanie blew on her lips and sighed.

Back in the Kinser Room, Melanie returned to the cutting station. Since she'd been gone, Rachel had disappeared, and Haley was back at the sewing machines. Melanie tackled a second outfit while she thought about what she'd overheard. Most guys would've loved receiving a girl like Bethany's attention. She was beautiful and rich. JB was definitely different, but it made more sense to her now.

In the pool, JB had mentioned he wouldn't date until he was older, but waiting until he was ready to get married? How long would that be? Definitely not in high school, probably even waiting until after college. That was a long time. It seemed a bit weird to her, too. But Melanie couldn't help but respect and admire him for his strong beliefs. She bit her lip. It made him even more likable.

Melanie tried to stifle a yawn. If she wasn't careful, she'd stick one of those pins right through her finger. Her eyelids drooped. She yawned again. She'd gotten up early for morning worship, and she'd expelled all that energy during dye wars. No wonder she was so tired.

Maybe she could finish the dress at home and take along some of the extra sheets to make bandages. When she made the suggestion to Bonnie and Jane, they agreed. Since she needed something to carry everything in, Melanie purchased two tote bags from the craft table. As she packed up the projects, her eyes wandered to the prayer cards for the missionaries. Sorting through the photos, Melanie chose a family like her own with two daughters. Shouldering her load, Melanie smiled. It felt so good to be making a difference.

21

FIRE CIRCLE

Dressed warmly against the night's chill, the campers gathered at the fire circle. Bonnie led them to an upper bench, where Melanie and her cabinmates huddled together under the canopy of stars. Orange flames blazed in the fire pit. A reverent silence captured them, interrupted only by the sounds of the popping and crackling of the burning logs. Holding a microphone, Eddie Jay stood on the cobblestones and asked them to share their testimonies about what God had done in their lives this week.

A figure shuffled uneasily from the first row. It was Adam. Eddie Jay passed him the microphone. Adam mumbled, and several people murmured they couldn't hear him. He started again. "All I wanted to say was that I know a lot of you were praying for me. And I just wanted to say thank you."

They clapped in response. Another person stepped up and then another. Each one had a different story about how God had reached out to them. A few more, including Cam, made their way to the front, creating a line.

When it was Cam's turn, he pushed up his glasses and gave a shaky smile. "Um, well, I'm up here so those in my youth group will keep me accountable, since I haven't been to church in a while. This week, I rededicated my life to Christ. I know I haven't really been faithful." He revealed some of his struggles. As he finished, Melanie and the other girls cheered for him.

As others spoke about how they'd been changed this week, Melanie's heart pounded. Her friends had said she should tell others she'd accepted Christ. She wiped her sweaty hands on her pants. Maybe this was her opportunity. Was she brave enough to do it?

She stood and scooted down the row. Being careful on the steps, she reached the end of the long line and waited for her turn. Her nervousness subsided when she listened to the others. Opening their hearts to each other brought a feeling of camaraderie like she'd sensed earlier today in morning worship. Was God drawing them all together?

Melanie bit her lip. *God, I don't really know what to say. But I'm grateful for what You've done for me, and I want to share it. Please help me.* Finally, it was her turn. Anxiety coursed through her, but she calmed as God's peace settled on her heart.

She stepped near the campfire and took a deep breath. "A few months ago, my family moved. I didn't know God, but I was really mad at Him for changing our lives. Then my mom and I started going to church, and I made some new friends."

Melanie continued, "I've been learning about God in youth group and that He wanted a relationship with me." She grinned broadly. "I realized He had been knocking on the door of my heart for a while. Yesterday, I made the decision to let Him in, and I accepted Jesus into my heart."

The audience cheered. Jumping up, Pastor Brett whooped and pumped his arm. Jane's screeching whistle penetrated the night. Most of the campers gave her a standing ovation. Even though she'd been nervous, the entire experience had filled her heart with joy.

As Melanie entered their row, each of the girls, including Bonnie, gave her a hug. Surrounded by her friends, she felt a bond, a connectedness, to them. An outpouring of happiness, love, and acceptance encompassed her. Could the others feel it, too? Overflowing with emotion, tears raced down her cheeks.

Melanie wiped off her face and settled back into her seat. Sensing someone watching her, she looked around. From the front row, JB beamed at her and sported a thumbs up. Melanie grinned and returned the gesture. He nodded.

The testimonies continued. Without Melanie noticing, Haley had gotten in line. When she stepped up, she confessed, "Actually, I don't know how to begin. I guess it starts with being adopted. I love my family, and I know my parents love me. They're here at camp, too. My dad is Pastor Cliff. I was sitting on his shoulders today during rec, and my mom, Jane, is the super loud whistler."

Jane whistled and a splatter of chuckling escaped the audience.

"Thanks, Mom. Anyway, I don't like telling people I'm adopted, even though it's obvious. Not because I'm ashamed—I'm proud of my family—it's just . . . " Her voice cracked. "It's just sometimes, people make it seem like we're not a *real* family. But we are."

More tears welled up in Melanie's eyes. Cindy sniffled next to her. Melanie's heart ached knowing others had hurt Haley. It was hard to remain in her seat, since she wanted to run up and comfort her friend. But she didn't want to be a distraction. This was about Haley.

"The other night, I was talking about this struggle with my friends. One of them has been watching the relationship I have with my parents and how much they love me. It helped her understand the truth of God's family and how we are all adopted into it. It's our real family. Later, she told me because of what I had shared, she decided to ask Jesus into her heart."

The crowd cheered and yelled. A few stood and clapped.

Haley took a deep breath. "Truthfully, I just wanted to say, we all go through struggles. But I've realized it is a testimony of what God is doing in our lives. And it's important to share it with others, even when it's uncomfortable. That's it." She shrugged.

After she finished, Haley practically ran up the aisle to her. Melanie moved to the end of the row. The two of them embraced.

Haley blurted, "I hope you don't mind that I shared about you."

Melanie replied, "How could I? It's *our* testimony."

"Oh, that's how I feel, too!" She squeezed Melanie again.

Melanie's heart soared. God was so good!

GOODBYE, CAMP REDWOODS

It had been a busy morning for Melanie with breakfast, packing up, and then trekking to the tabernacle with her suitcase and all her things. Because of the craft projects, she had two extra bags to take home. The campgrounds were a hive of activity. Sitting on the edge of the planter at the roundhouse, Melanie and the rest of her friends waited for Bonnie, Rachel, and Bethany so they could take pictures together.

Melanie moaned. "I can't believe this is our last day. Do we have to go home?"

Katie sighed in understanding. "Unfortunately, yes. But, hey, at least we get to spend the rest of the weekend together, and we have Cindy's birthday party tomorrow."

"Oh, I almost forgot." Melanie pursed her lips, hiding a sly smile.

Cindy playfully slapped her arm. "Hey, that's not nice."

Melanie's eyes widened. "Ouch! I was just kidding." She continued, "But seriously, I have a question or two about last night. Eddie Jay mentioned we'd be taking communion. What is that? And what am I supposed to do?"

Cindy tilted her head. "Communion is a way we express as born-again Christians that we believe and accept Jesus' gift to us of our salvation."

"Wow, Cin! That's such a deep and spiritual answer," Haley retorted. "Mermaid, it's just showing God and others what we believe."

"You're both right, but it's more than that. Let me think." Katie hummed. "Mel, communion is an outward sign that you've asked Jesus into your heart and acknowledge He died on the cross for you. It's also a time of reflection, where we focus on confessing our sins, especially if we are holding something against another believer."

"Nooooo." Cindy groaned. "Now you're making me feel bad about what happened with Bethany."

Katie leaned her head forward. "I didn't do it intentionally."

Haley sighed. "It's something we're all going to have to think about."

Melanie scrunched her forehead. "I don't understand. Bethany was wrong. Do you mean you're going to forgive her without her saying she's sorry?"

The girls nodded.

Ella explained, "It's more than forgiveness. We have to let go of our anger. Truthfully, it's not really about Bethany. It's about our heart attitude—how we respond to her."

Cindy shook her head. "It feels like a balancing act because she shouldn't treat us the way she does, but God still wants us to show her His love." She chuckled. "I don't know if I'm up for the challenge."

Haley agreed. "Yeah, you're not the only one."

Melanie blew on her lips. "Wow, I have a lot to learn. Being a Christian isn't easy."

"Not always. It seems like we're throwing you into the deep end," Haley said.

Melanie teased, "Don't worry about it. I'm a good swimmer. Remember, I'm a mermaid. And because of you guys, I already know some of the advantages of having Christ in my life. I mean, I have friends like you."

Katie put her arm around Melanie's shoulder. "We're more than friends now; we're officially family, remember?"

Melanie nodded.

Later, in the gym for Tab Time, Eddie Jay spoke reverently as he explained about communion. Melanie was so thankful her friends had told her about what it meant and what to expect. Carrying trays of crackers, the guy counselors walked slowly up the aisles. The silver tray was passed down the row. Melanie grabbed one and passed it on. The cracker in her hand made her feel like she was part of something, something bigger than herself.

Thank You, Jesus, for dying on the cross for me to cover all my sins.

When Eddie Jay indicated, Melanie ate the cracker in unison with everyone else. Next, they passed out the grape juice. Melanie was even more careful as she lifted the cup from the tray and handed it to Katie. The overhead lights reflected in the juice. It reminded Melanie of Jesus' light shining in the darkness.

Thank You, Jesus, for shedding Your blood for me.

Again, they took communion together.

***

Melanie sat alone at the lunch table. Bowing her head, she prayed, *Dear God, Thank You for this food. Thank You for giving me the opportunity to come here and have such a great time. Help me to learn more about You and that Bonnie and I can do the discipleship together. Also, God, I really want Dad and Megan to have a relationship with You, too.* She heard noise around her and closed with a quick amen.

Melanie glanced around at her friends. As always, Katie had taken the seat next to her, and Cindy sat on her other side. Haley and Ella were elbowing each other across from her. The rest of their cabin joined them. Her heart was pulled in two different directions. She wished camp could go on forever, but she also missed her family. She couldn't wait to tell them everything. And she missed playing with her new parakeet, Paco.

Haley groaned. "I hate to leave. We'll have to wait a whole year to come back."

Rachel piped in, "Not for Bethany and me since we'll be in high school. No more junior high camp for us. Next Sunday, we will be graduating into 4TK."

Katie asked, "What's 4TK?"

Ella volunteered, "It's the name of the high school youth group. It stands for 'For the King.'"

Bethany eyed Melanie. "JB will be going in there, too."

Haley snorted. "Don't forget Adam."

Melanie wouldn't be sorry to see Bethany and Adam go, but she would definitely miss Rachel in God's Rock and also JB. Would Cam be moving up, too? Who else would be graduating into 4TK? But that would also mean they'd be getting some new kids in youth group.

After lunch, Melanie exited the dining hall with her friends. At the stairs, she stopped. Her parents were here! Melanie's heart gave a jolt. Her dad stood in the exact spot at the fire circle where she had shared her testimony last night. *Oh, God, I want my dad to know You, too. Please let my light shine, so he will see You.*

She clambered down the steps with Katie, Cindy, Haley, and Ella trailing behind her. At the bottom, she raced around the corner and threw her arms around her dad.

He squeezed her tight. "We've missed you! It's been a long week."

Mom sat in her wheelchair. Her eyes glistened with tears. "Mel, I'm so happy."

Melanie knew what she meant and smiled. Leaning over, she embraced her mom and whispered, "I can't wait to tell you everything."

Katie and the rest of the girls greeted her parents. Then it was time to leave. In the tabernacle, Melanie directed her dad to her and Katie's suitcases. Melanie grabbed the two tote bags. Her friends retrieved their own things and headed to the parking lot.

Outside, Mom insisted on having the totes on her lap, while Melanie wheeled her along the path. Mom peeked inside them, inspecting the contents.

"Mom, be careful. I don't want you to get pricked. There's pins in one of those."

"What's in here?" Mom asked, slightly alarmed.

Melanie giggled. "That's a part of the everything I was going to share with you. They're missionary projects—crafts we can do to help others. We're going to have so much fun!"

At the bus, the kids from church were loading up. Bonnie stood with her clipboard like she had on the first day. Thankfully, seeing Bonnie reminded Melanie the important question she wanted to ask her mom. She'd almost forgotten.

Melanie gasped. "Oh, Mom, can Bonnie disciple me? Would that be okay?"

"Of course!" Mom reached back and patted her hand. "And when we get to the car, drop me off so you can go and say a proper goodbye to your friends."

Next to the bus, Melanie and Katie hugged Cindy, Haley, and Ella. Seeing Rachel already inside, Melanie waved to her. Ella hustled up the steps and Haley followed.

Cindy beamed. "We'll see you guys tomorrow for my birthday party."

"Can't wait," Melanie and Katie said together and laughed. Katie returned to the car.

Melanie walked over to Bonnie. "Bonnie, my mom said you can disciple me."

"That's great, Mel. I'll call you so we can arrange a time, but you can start the reading. We'll be studying the book of John. Read the first chapter and write down any questions you have."

"Got it. I will. I think I'm going to enjoy this kind of homework."

"You'll learn a lot."

"And, Bonnie, thank you so much for everything."

"No problem. It was definitely a pleasure."

Melanie hugged her.

As their car exited the parking lot, Melanie turned and peered out the back window. She was going to miss this place, since so many wonderful things had happened to her here. This was the best week of her life, one she would never forget. Her life had been changed forever. She sighed in contentment. *Goodbye, Camp Redwoods. You will always have a cherished place in my heart.*

The Romans Road

The Romans Road is a series of verses (listed below) which lay out God's plan of salvation.

Romans 3:23: "For all have sinned and fall short of the glory of God."

Romans 6:23: "For the wages of sin is death, but the gracious gift of God is eternal life in Christ Jesus our Lord."

Romans 5:8: "But God demonstrates His own love toward us, in that while we were still sinners, Christ died for us."

Romans 10:9-10: "That if you confess with your mouth Jesus *as* Lord, and believe in your heart that God raised Him from the dead, you will be saved; for with the heart *a person* believes, resulting in righteousness, and with the mouth he confesses, resulting in salvation."

Romans 10:13: "For 'EVERYONE WHO CALLS ON THE NAME OF THE LORD WILL BE SAVED.'"

We have all sinned, and we deserve death. But God provided a way through Jesus to save us. He died on the cross for our sins and was raised from the dead. If you believe this and want to ask Jesus to be your Lord and Savior, here is a simple prayer: *Dear Lord Jesus, I know that I am a sinner, and I ask for Your forgiveness. I believe You died for my sins and rose from the dead. I invite You to come into my heart, and I want You to be Lord of my life. In Jesus' name, Amen.*

If you prayed that prayer, I'm so glad that you've accepted Jesus into your heart. Welcome to God's family. God has made you a new creation. To begin your new life, it is important to learn more about your faith and grow in your walk with the Lord. We call this discipleship. The first steps are to read your Bible and find a Bible-believing church to attend.

Please let me know if you have made a decision to follow Christ and if you need any guidance. You can contact me through my website at jdrempel.com.

Discussion Questions

Chapter 1

1. If you were to go on a trip, what would you take with you?
2. Are there responsibilities you need taken care of when you're away?
3. Do you have your own Bible?
4. Do you know someone who is adopted?
5. If you do know someone who is adopted, how does their family treat them?

Chapter 2

1. Was Bethany dressed appropriately for camp?
2. When Bethany insulted Cindy, what would have been a better response?
3. Even though Cindy is upset about Bethany's comment, was it right for Cindy to say something to Melanie about it? Why or why not?

4. Why is it important to pray before you go on a trip?

Chapter 3

1. Have you ever gone to youth camp with your friends? If so, what did you enjoy most?
2. What are missionaries? Do you know anyone who is a missionary?
3. Has there been a place you've visited that filled you with wonder and excitement?
4. When you see the beauty of nature, how does it make you feel about God?
5. What do you think "Light of the World" means?

Chapter 4

1. Have you ever gone camping? Did you stay in a cabin or a tent?
2. What do you think Melanie was anticipating would happen at camp?
3. Is there a special place you go with your family often?
4. What do you like about your special place?
5. Rachel talks about keeping their cabin clean. Would this be difficult for you?

Chapter 5

1. Is it okay to keep secrets? When is keeping a secret wrong?
2. If you went to camp, what would you want to see first?
3. Do you agree with the girls that Bethany was being snobby?
4. Should the girls be talking about Bethany behind her back? Why or why not?

Chapter 6

1. Have you ever lied unintentionally? What happened?
2. Did you know lying is a sin?
3. How did Jesus conquer sin and death?
4. Did you know that Jesus died for you?

Chapter 7

1. What challenges did the girls encounter as a team?
2. Is it wrong to pull a prank like the boys did trying to scare the girls? Why or why not?
3. Did you suspect Jane as a "hidden" counselor?
4. Jane answered her daughter's question honestly, but was she still lying? Why or why not?

Chapter 8

1. Do you have soulo time/quiet time with God every day?
2. What do you do during your soulo time/quiet time with God?
3. Have you ever praised God despite doing something you didn't like?
4. Why did the janitor sing praises to God?
5. Which game of rec would you like best?

Chapter 9

1. Have you ever made a promise to God? What was it? Did you keep it?
2. Whose fault was it that Melanie's lie was repeated—Bethany or Melanie's?
3. What were the consequences of Melanie's lie?

Chapter 10

1. Do you think Bethany was being a showoff posing in the pictures? Why?
2. Do you enjoy singing praise songs?
3. How can someone be a light to the world?
4. How does Jesus live inside us?
5. How have you shown kindness to others?

Chapter 11

1. Have you ever lost something you needed?
2. Have you ever done something that was difficult or made you nervous? How did you feel afterwards?
3. Have you ever encouraged a friend who was doubting themselves?
4. Have you been a friend to someone who isn't liked by others?

Chapter 12

1. Are there any clichés you use?
2. What makes you unique?
3. Have you ever done something challenging?
4. Have you ever been envious of someone? How did you get over it?

Chapter 13

1. What is the difference between making a decision and rededicating your life to God?
2. What is the main reason to ask Jesus into your heart? (Hint: It shouldn't be to please people.)
3. When Jesus wants to dine with us, it means He seeks fellowship with us. How can you have fellowship with Him?

4. Did you know that God loves you and cares about you? He wants you to be His child. If you would like to be His child, go to "The Romans Road" page for instructions.

5. What made Melanie like Bethany?

Chapter 14

1. What are the similarities between the relationship Haley has with her parents and our relationship to God?

2. Have you been adopted into God's family?

3. What prompted Melanie to ask Jesus into her heart?

4. Do you have a relationship with Jesus? If not and you would like to, go to "The Romans Road" page for instructions.

5. When you accepted Jesus into your heart, who was the very first person you wanted to tell?

Chapter 15

1. If you accepted Jesus into your heart, was it so that you could go to Heaven or because you loved Jesus? Or both?

2. Have you cried because you were so happy?

3. How has God answered your prayers? If so, what was it?

4. Why is it important to remember the date you accepted Jesus into your heart?

5. If you've asked Jesus into your heart, have people noticed a difference in you?

Chapter 16

1. Do you have a favorite spot where you feel close to God?

2. Do you have a friend like Katie who prays for you?

3. Has someone shown you the light and love of Jesus?

4. If you know Jesus, have you been a light to others? If yes, how so? If not, what can you do to show others that Jesus loves them?

Chapter 17

1. Did the girls have the right attitude about Adam being the one who was hurt?

2. Do you have a talent you would share at a talent show?

3. How do you keep from being frightened when you have to face an audience?

4. Is it important to pursue being famous? Why or why not?

5. Is someone really your friend if they make fun of you? What is the difference between teasing and making fun of someone?

6. After the mean things Bethany did, if she were your friend, would you continue to be hers? Why or why not?

7. Why do you think Rachel is upset with herself and Cindy?

8. What do you think are some of the difficulties Bethany faces in her every-day life?

Chapter 18

1. What is discipleship?

2. If you know Jesus as your Savior, have you been discipled?

3. Are you involved in any ministries or outreach projects?

4. What is something you can do for others?

5. What would you do if you ever had to stand up against one of your friends who was doing wrong?

6. What should Rachel have done in the situation?

Chapter 19

1. Have you ever participated in dye wars?
2. Would you feel sorry for Adam since he didn't get to participate in dye wars?
3. Were you surprised Adam didn't get Ella back for getting him wet?

Chapter 20

1. Do you have a skill someone might be surprised to learn about you?
2. Have you taught someone else your skill?
3. Have you made a difference in someone else's life?
4. Bethany seems to be obsessed with JB and follows him around everywhere. Is this appropriate behavior? Why or why not?
5. Do you respect and admire JB for standing up for his beliefs? Why?

Chapter 21

1. Do you get nervous speaking in front of a group of people?
2. What is a testimony?
3. Do you have a testimony of what God has done in your life?

4. Would you be willing to share your testimony with others?
5. What is a "real" family?
6. If you accepted Jesus into your heart, how do you feel about being adopted into God's family?

Chapter 22

1. Would you be willing to forgive Bethany if she was your friend?
2. What does it mean to be a part of God's family?
3. What is Communion?
4. Have you ever participated in taking Communion?
5. Is there someone in your life you want to come into a relationship with Jesus? Pray for that person.
6. Have you read the book of John? If you are a new believer, it's a great place to start learning about your faith.

Acknowledgments

Over the last two years of writing *Melanie at Camp Redwoods*, there are many I would like to thank for their help, encouragement, and support:

- My Father God, Who challenged me with one of the hardest tasks He has asked me to do. I'm thankful that He walked beside me and guided me.
- My husband, Matt, whose love and constant support has made my dreams a reality
- My family, specifically Mommy, Poppy, Sissy, Trevor, Claudia, Geri, Mom and Dad Rempel, Aunt Sue, Uncle Marv, and the rest of my extended family, who love, support, and cheer for me
- Ambassador International—Sam, Anna, Daphne, Katie, Hannah, Susanna, and Bethany—for believing in me and for your help in the creation of *Melanie at Camp Redwoods*

- James L. Rubart, my writing coach/mentor and friend, for being such a blessing to work with and such a gifted encourager.
- Julie Harbison, cherished friend, fellow author, encourager, and your professional fangirl
- Pastor Ed (the real "Eddie Jay") and Maria Crable, who supported me and provide me a cherished friendship that has meant more to me than I can describe. You've been a great blessing in my life.
- Jim Blake for his dedication to Alliance Redwoods and for giving me permission to use ARCG as the backdrop for *Melanie at Camp Redwoods*
- Caitlyn Bishop, whose continued help made this book possible
- ARCG staff —for their dedication in serving those who visit Alliance Redwoods
- Susan Bollinger, alpha reader, editor, and sweet friend
- Deanna Carlton, encourager and cherished friend
- Cady Crider, encourager and friend
- Pastor Greg Jack who has left a lasting legacy in my heart and in the hearts of others, and

to Maria, his wonderful wife, who loved,
encouraged, and supported him in his ministry

- My Hillside Alliance Church family
- Oregon Christian Writers for your ministry
  to writers
- Devoted readers and parents of *The NorCal Girls*
  series for your encouragement and reviews

Donate

The NorCal Girls series was inspired by my family trips to camp. We spent many wonderful summers at Alliance Redwood Conference Grounds. A portion of the proceeds from this series will be donated toward ARCG's general fund and scholarship fund so other kids can go to camp. You can donate, too, at www.allianceredwoods.com/give.

Christian camps need our help, so please consider donating to them. We need to work together to save these wonderful places, which spread the news of Jesus Christ and provide a place where we can learn more about Him.

For more information about

J.D. Rempel
and
Melanie at Camp Redwoods
please connect:

www.jdrempel.com
www.facebook.com/jdrempel
@jdrempelwriter
www.instagram.com/j.d.rempel

For more information about
AMBASSADOR INTERNATIONAL
please connect:

www.ambassador-international.com
@AmbassadorIntl
www.facebook.com/AmbassadorIntl

*If you enjoyed this book, please consider leaving us a review on
Amazon, Goodreads, or our website.*

I Want a Water Buffalo for Christmas tells the journey of LeGory, a young water buffalo, who brings life to a family in dire need. Several circumstances fall into place to create the life-giving wonder of providing for those less fortunate.

Everyone has to deal with a bully at some point in life, and it can be really, really hard! Come tag along on an adventure in Laurel Wood and see how a young otter named Elliot Emerson, or E.E. for short, and his gang of friends square off with a group of bullfrog bullies on the basketball court at Dogwood Park.

For Chris, aka "Meatloaf," it's all about brains. If you can see it, you can believe it. If it's logical, it's true. If it's scientific, then it's trustworthy.

When invisible air creatures start crawling around on him, his entire view of life gets upended, and the Maker opens Meatloaf's eyes and heart to the possibility that there is a Maker of the world and the universe after all.